Love in Rio
Love and Travel Series

Book 2

Misty Rosette

Copyright © Misty Rosette

CONTENTS

CHAPTER 1

The constant race between the sun and the moon for dominion over the sky means the days come and go quickly. This gets even worse when you ask the universe for some more time; when you need just a little more time to be with the ones you love. Chloe had these thoughts each time Francis came to New York. The clock always began to tick faster, flying almost at breakneck speed and robbing her of the time she had to spend with her man.

Tonight, she was trying not to think about the fact that he would be leaving again the next day. Over the past week, she had thought constantly about where their relationship might be heading, about what it meant to both of them, especially since he was never around. She wanted to place all of her focus on the show that she had convened on behalf of Galantino couture; they would be displaying some designer items, and for the first time in a long time, she would be walking the runway instead of just hanging in the background as the organizer.

Her mind returned to Francis. The fact that he would be there, in the audience, meant everything to her. For the first time since they had started dating, he would be present to watch her do her thing.

Francis was a doctor and worked with Doctors Without Borders, traveling around the world to provide medical services to people in disadvantaged places. Chloe loved that he was giving back to the world, but she hated that his desire to give came in the way of what they had. She had met him at Olivia's wedding; he happened to be in the same circle as Antonio and Carlo. Carlo was Olivia's husband.

They had clicked immediately. Something about him had completely charmed Chloe, and he was as smitten as she had been. They had begun a whirlwind romance that threatened to swallow them up, until he had to leave for Senegal. This was the second time she was seeing him in the past year, and it was breaking her heart that he would be leaving again in a little over forty-eight hours. She had spoken to the girls about a week before about how she felt what they had kindled in the first few months had died or grown dull in the face of the constant absence.

"How's the communication when he travels?" Olivia had asked.

"Sometimes he visits places where there's no reception, and we end up not speaking for a month," Chloe had replied.

"Wow, wow," Ava had exclaimed.

"Wait, how's the romance when he returns to New York from his trips?" Avery had asked.

"Well, it's always fire! We're literally burning for each other, but then he leaves, and I'm back where I was a few days before," Chloe had complained.

"That can't be easy for you," Olivia had quipped, squeezing Chloe's hand.

Chloe wanted to have a chat about all of this with Francis, to tell him how she really felt and how lonely she got whenever he was away, but it never seemed like a good time to bring something like that up. Sometimes, she worried about what he would become if she asked him to quit his passion and come open a practice in New York. He had said that was in his plans, but it would be another thing if she demanded that he return to New York for her. They had only been dating for a year.

She grabbed her phone from her bag and sent him a quick text. The show would be up and running in an hour; he should have been there already. "Where are you, sweetness?" He called her sweetness, and she had taken to calling him that too, an endearing term that she couldn't seem to get enough of. Each time he used it, she felt her heart do a little flip and a smile crease the sides of her face.

She didn't get a reply to her text, and she didn't send another. Organizing these events was always like a madhouse for Chloe; there was always too much to do to make sure everything didn't crumble at the worst possible moment. In that particular moment, she was thinking more about the success of her event than the presence of her man.

"Hey, hey," Mia called, making her way into the backstage room where Chloe and the other models were getting ready.

"Hey, Mia," Chloe called, reaching out to hug her friend. She paused and looked behind Mia, and her eyebrows rose slightly. "Wait, you came alone?"

"No, Liv and the others are still looking for a good place to park. I snuck off so I could see you in your dress first!" Mia laughed.

"Oh, I'm sorry, I won't be dressed until everyone else is dressed," Chloe explained.

"That's okay. Is Francis here yet?" Mia asked.

"I'm not sure. If he is, I'm sure he'll be in the studio; he's like that, says he wouldn't want to jinx it by seeing me while I'm doing my thing," Chloe explained. Mia didn't say a word. If she said what she wanted to say, it would be something about how his presence would act as a boost and not a jinx to anything. But it wasn't her place, and she was sure this wasn't the time to mention something like that. The others came in at that moment with wide eyes and smiley faces.

"You guys, thank you for coming," Chloe said, pulling them into a warm embrace.

"We wouldn't miss this for the world! Do you know the last time you walked the runway?" Olivia asked.

"I'm sure you're going to own it today," Ava stated. "These young girls don't know who you are," she added. Chloe blew air kisses at them, smiling broadly. This circle of women had always been her backbone. They were always there to support each other in good times and bad.

She went about her business, moving from one end of the room to another, making sure everything was in order. She didn't have time to think of the man in her life, but somewhere in her mind, she knew she wanted him to be out there in the crowd. She wanted to have his eyes on her when she walked down the runway. Two hundred people would be out there among the audience, but she kept her eye out for only one. And even now, she wasn't sure he would be there.

When each of the models had walked the runway, she walked down as the final piece, wearing a flannel jumpsuit with a perfect slit around the neck. Her steps were gracious as she bounced on her feet, strolling with the confidence of a seasoned model as she made her way along the runway. She could hear the voices of her friends as they screamed, hailing her entrance onto the fashion scene after a long hiatus. In the past year, all she had done was arrange these events; she was never featured. She had chosen to keep to the background, but after a long break, the hunger to be at the center was once again coming back to the fore.

She looked out for Francis, her eyes staring into the crowd in search of her man. But he wasn't there. Her excitement died, and she became all business, walking with steady and elegant gait, one hand on her waist. When she posed at the edge of the walkway, her eyes sought Francis once more. She could feel the slip even before it even happened; when her knees knocked together on her turn, she put out her hands before falling on them. She didn't wait to hear the 'ooohs' from the audience; she rose with grace and marched off the stage.

As she walked the runway for the final lap, her eyes caught a face in the crowd. She took a second look at it once again. It was a face too familiar yet without a name attached to it. She wondered where she had crossed paths with the individual. He had an indulgent smile; one that seemed to be applauding even though his hands weren't moving. She smiled at her friends and turned stylishly, making her way back into the dressing room, trying to bury her error.

When she emerged at the parking lot afterward, leaving her workers to wrap things up, her ladies were waiting by the car for her. She fell into their arms, happy for their support.

"You were fire, girl!" Olivia quipped. Liv was the one who held most of them together with a cool head. Chloe brought the fire and feistiness, ready to fight for her friends at any moment. These two always seemed to prominently lead the group.

"It could have been better. Francis should have been here," Chloe said. "I'm not blaming him for anything. I'm just saying."

"Has he said anything?" Ava asked.

"Not a word!" Chloe fumed.

"He might have left a voicemail. You have been pretty busy all day, remember?" Avery suggested.

Chloe whipped her phone out of her pocket and stared at the screen for a second. She keyed in her code and opened her voicemail; he had left one. Her first thought was to delete it without listening. There was nothing to be said. But she knew she should listen. She opened it with her friends there, leaving it on speaker.

"Hi, sweetness. I'm sorry I won't be able to make it to your thing tonight. Some of the doctors from my program came to town this evening. They're having a conference tomorrow and wanted to hang out tonight. I couldn't say no. I'm sure you'll kill it out there! I'll see you when you get back."

When his voice and the ambient noise faded out, they were all quiet, staring at the tips of their shoes or up into the dark sky bereft of stars. There were no words, not for this. Mia laid a hand on Chloe's shoulder, providing support. Chloe felt a mixture of anger and disappointment.

"We should get going," Chloe said. "Would you mind dropping me off at my apartment, Liv?" she asked.

"Not at all. Come on," Olivia said.

"Hello. Excuse me, Chloe Baxter?" a deep masculine voice called out. They all turned, looking to see who it was. Chloe squinted, recognizing the face she had caught amongst the crowd when she had walked the runway. She still couldn't tell where she had seen that face, but she knew she had encountered it before now.

"That was an excellent performance in there. You talked about being involved in the fashion world, but I didn't know you were this active in it," he said with a wide smile, walking up with an outstretched hand toward Chloe. She was still skeptical. It was at that moment that her memory came flying back, and a name popped up for the face.

"William!" she called, and opened her arms to him. He hugged her and lingered a little. When they broke the hug, she stood staring at him with a big smile on her face. "What are you doing in New York?" she queried.

"Well, I'm on a short leave. Heard about this event with a familiar name attached, and I figured I should come and see your magic. And I am wowed! Wowed!" he quipped, smiling broadly. Chloe stared at his dimpled cheek, which seemed to be pressed in further by something when he smiled. She wondered why it took her so long to recognize him.

"It's been a year! Or even more!" Chloe said, her voice laden with accusation.

"I'm sorry. I spent the past year trying to help quell the conflict in Yemen. I would have called, but that place is not a haven from which one can maintain contact with ease," he apologized, smiling and stretching out his hand to touch her shoulder again.

Her ladies crowded her, looking to get some form of introduction. She rolled her eyes at them and turned to William, who still wore a smile on his face.

"William, these are my friends: Olivia, Mia, Ava, and Avery." she said. "You guys remember the guy who singed my skin with hot coffee at the airport in LA? This is him." She chuckled.

"Oh, come on, that's not fair. I apologized," he defended himself.

"That makes it all go away completely." Chloe laughed.

They chatted for a little while, and William took her number again, promising to call her later. The ladies talked nonstop about his pretty face and muscular features on the ride home. No one recalled the no-show Francis. But Olivia, sharp as a blade, was the one who pointed out that Chloe might be attracting too many guys who were not fixed to a specific location.

"We should probably get you a man with his life in this ole city of ours." She winked.

"William is just an acquaintance," Chloe defended.

"A friend who wants to be more than that!" Mia, with penetrating eyes, chipped in.

"Mia has said it all. And you know when she calls it, she knows what she's saying," Ava concurred.

"Whatever. I don't know what you are all saying. I just need some good sleep, so I know what to do with Francis when he pulls up at my door in the morning," Chloe stated.

"Do you need any help? You just have to call, and I'm out there. I can throw hands," Avery, the one with another wild streak, stated. They were all smiling as they pulled up to Chloe's.

CHAPTER 2

The sun was petering off into the dark western horizon when Chloe pulled up to her apartment. She received a call from the directors of Galantino couture, who had contracted her for the event. They needed a quick meeting, and she was happy to keep busy. When she grabbed her phone from her purse later in the evening, there were about twelve missed calls. Ten were from Francis, while the other two were from an unknown number. It was probably Francis trying to reach her through another number. She opened her voicemail; he had left about five in there. She quickly deleted them without listening.

She was tired. It didn't take much to make an effort, and he wasn't showing her even the slightest bit of it in this relationship of theirs. Their animal magnetism aside, she couldn't point to a single part of their relationship that made her feel as good as she would like to.

She saw him before she even parked her car. He was standing with his face looking repentant. She parked the car, stepped out, and walked toward her apartment. He was standing with his legs up against the wall. He stood straight when he saw her walking up.

"I've been trying to reach you, sweetness," he said, reaching out for her hand. She let him take it, his eyes staring into hers as he began to speak. Her phone rang in that moment; it was the other number that had called her earlier. She had thought it was just Francis trying to reach her, but now he was standing right there before her while the same number was calling. She clicked the button and brought the phone up to her ear.

"Hello?" she asked, ignoring the look on Francis's face.

"Hey, Chloe. Will here. I've been trying to reach you," he said.

"Oh, Will!" she exclaimed with excitement on her face. "How are you?"

"I'm well. Are you doing alright?" he asked.

"Yes. I'm sorry. I've been in a meeting for most of the day. I'm only just returning to my apartment now," she replied.

"Give me the address, and I'll come pick you up for an evening of peaceful fun," he said.

"I'm not sure, Will. I'm a little tired," she said.

"Trust me, I know exactly what you need at this point," he said.

"Okay, give me fifteen minutes to freshen up," she said. "I'll text you my address right away."

She turned to walk into her apartment and found Francis standing there, glowering at her. He looked really angry.

"What were you saying, Francis?" she asked.

"So you can really be this disrespectful? I was speaking to you, and all you could think about doing was talking on the phone with another guy? Who was that, anyway?" he asked.

"You chose your doctor friends over me, Francis. I'm choosing myself over you," Chloe replied.

"They just came into town and will only be staying for a day at most. I couldn't just abandon them. What would you have me do?" he asked.

"Nothing, absolutely nothing. Can I go in now?" she asked.

"So you're using that as an excuse for your promiscuity?" he asked.

"Get off this porch this moment, Francis!" she yelled, staring him down. She didn't say another word; she didn't have to. The fire in her eyes was enough to let Francis know there was nothing to negotiate. He ambled off, and she watched him go, wondering how one could be so irresponsible yet demand accountability. She should have seen this coming a long time ago, but she wasn't paying attention. He loved his job more than anything else in the world; even the woman in his life meant less than it did. That may not be a bad thing, but it wasn't something Chloe was willing to deal with.

William pulled up a few minutes later, parked, and stepped out of his car. He was wearing a blue T-shirt and black denim pants. She saw him from her apartment and watched his broad shoulders held in a tight embrace by the T-shirt. He rested his back against the frame of his car, looking dapper in casual clothes.

She walked toward him, beaming a smile in his direction as she stepped down the stairs. He smiled as she approached.

"Well, if this is your tired face, I wonder what you look like when you aren't tired," he commented.

"Well, a little touch-up always hides some of the tiredness around the eyes," she said.

"You must be some sort of miracle worker then," he said. "Come on, let me help you unwind a little," he said, leading her over to the passenger side and opening the door. She slipped in, whispering her thanks as he closed the door for her.

He drove through the city, making his way through 82nd and 104th on the Upper East Side. He parked in front of a tall high-rise building and stepped out, walking around to open the door for her again. She stepped out, wearing a huge smile on her face.

"You know, you could have told me you were taking me to see art," she said as she stepped out of the car.

"Do you not love art?" he asked.

"Well, I do love art, and I wouldn't have said no to the beauty on this street, not in the least," she replied.

"Well, while there is a lot of art on this street, we didn't come here to look at it. There's more to life than the aesthetics of art." He smiled and took her hand, leading her to an elevator in the lobby of the high-rise building. They sailed up to the twenty-third floor, his hand holding hers tight.

She loved the possessiveness of the gesture, and the fact that he was offering her an opportunity to rise out of the doldrums of heartbreak, but she hoped he wouldn't expect more than she was willing to give. Jumping out of an ill-fated relationship with Francis only to jump into another with William was simply a recipe for disaster, and she wouldn't allow herself to make such a mistake.

He led her through a hallway, still holding her hand. It felt tender while remaining possessive without words or overt action. They walked to the end of the room, and he knocked lightly on a metal door. A small panel slid back on the door.

"Identify yourself!" a voice called.

"Sergeant Hanley, Foxtrot Alpha," William said, putting his lips close to the door. Chloe watched with a small smile on her lips as the door slid open and William grabbed her hand again, leading her into a large space with several tables arranged in a perfect square. People sat in groups of two or more, drinking beer and eating. Soft music wafted out of the wall speakers, which made Chloe smile. She had never learned to be indifferent when Adele's music came floating into her ears. She wondered why a bunch of soldiers would be listening to Adele though. Suddenly she heard gunshots, and loud calls to "take cover" came over the speakers. Her heart jumped within her, but William's hand on hers calmed her down and made her relax.

"What is this place?" she asked as he led her to a table and made to pull a seat out for her to sit in. She lowered herself into the seat, and he slid it back in for her. When he sat, he laid his hands on the table and smiled at her.

"This used to be a safe house in the old days. Well, not this room exactly. But several years ago, there was a stucco building standing where this high-rise now stands. And in that small stucco building, the army often housed some of the men returning from the war fronts, men who weren't ready to head home yet. That was when Uncle Sam still cared for soldiers returning home from the fronts. This was their safe haven, the spot where they prepared themselves for returning home because it's hard to come directly home from a battlefield. It takes a little while to readjust."

The waiter came, but William wouldn't let Chloe order. He whispered an order into the waiter's ear that Chloe couldn't make out. He did allow her to choose between red and white wine. When the waiter was gone, he turned to her quickly.

"I'm sorry if I was a little too forward there. I should have told you sooner; Chef Montes is a Hispanic gentleman in charge of the kitchen here, and he serves medium-rare ribs that will set your taste buds on fire. That's just about the best thing in the building," he said.

"Oh, now I get it. I would love to taste what Chef Montes has to offer," she said, smiling. "Now, complete that bit of history you were sharing with me." She winked, taken by the tale. She liked everything with a bit of history; it made things more relatable.

"A couple of soldiers gathered and decided to make this room a throwback to that time in history. While it's not a live-in space, it offers returning soldiers the same atmosphere as the war fronts, helping them feel like they are back there so that they can gradually loose the grip of the fronts," he said.

"How does that help with PTSD?" Chloe asked.

"Sometimes a man needs to know that there are others going through the same things; it helps them understand that they are not made-up. There is also a little gathering held here twice a week where men get to speak to others going through the same issues, which helps them to heal," William replied. His beeper went off, and he looked down at his belt, staring for a moment at the small digital screen. His face colored slightly, and Chloe looked away, realizing what that look stood for.

Their meal came just at the right time, and William rubbed his palms together in anticipation. He grabbed his fork and cut through the meat, biting a small piece and smiling at the deliciousness of Montes's meals. The taste never changed like some chefs were wont to do with their cuisine. He paused and watched Chloe's face, waiting to see her reaction when she took her first bite of the meat. She cut into it slowly, then teased him with laughter as she bit into it. Her brows rose, questioning what she tasted.

"Oh my God," she exclaimed.

"Right? Right?" He laughed, clapping both of his hands together.

"It just melts in your mouth like butter. Is this meat? Is this really meat?" she quipped, taking another quick bite and giggling like a schoolgirl as she bit into it. "Oh my God, I love it!" she exclaimed.

"I told you," he said.

They spent a few hours there. Chloe easily got used to the shouts and gunshots intermittently coming over the speakers thanks to William's stoicism. He led her down the stairs afterward, choosing them over the elevator this time. He took her hand as they walked. For a while, they enjoyed some silence.

"I couldn't help but notice a tinge of sadness in your eyes earlier when I came over to your apartment," he mentioned.

"It's nothing. Just a little matter of the heart," she said.

"I'm sorry," he said.

"Don't be. It's the best thing for me," she replied.

He drove her back home. It was late when they arrived, and he wondered out loud if she had had plans for the day that he might have messed up.

"No. I had a series of meetings today, but my calendar is free tomorrow, so I can get all the rest I need or work if I wish to," she said.

"Unfortunately for me, I won't be here to possibly take advantage of your free day," he said.

"Is everything okay?" she asked.

"Yes, everything is fine. I'm headed back to work. My team is being summoned to Rio de Janeiro. There is a little conflict developing over there, and I am to join up for a peace-keeping mission," he said.

"But you said you were here for a month?" she asked.

"The army sometimes cares very little about what we really want to do with our time. They call and expect us to answer," he explained. "I'm sorry. I was really hoping to get to know you on this vacation. I came to New York specifically to get a good dose of you," he explained.

"Don't worry. I'm used to people leaving. It's not your fault," she said, tapping his shoulder softly before walking up to her apartment. She didn't look back; she didn't try to. This was the story:

They come. They make her feel like they might be staying. Then they leave. This wasn't much different from Francis, except that William was actually being summoned. There was also the fact that she hadn't fallen head over heels for William. Not yet, anyway. It would have felt much worse if she had spent more time with him, only for him to be uprooted from her life again.

CHAPTER 3

The summer always brought some happiness for Chloe. It meant she could head out on a new adventure, see a new place, and learn something new. She had been doing this with her ladies for the past three years, and each year found them enjoying the beauty of a new clime and a new culture. This year, it felt even more needed. She would love to escape from New York, go to a new place, and try to wash off the bad luck she seemed to be having with the men in her life.

It had been three months since she called it quits with Francis. He had returned to some Asian country to do his Doctors Without Borders bit, and only last month, he posted a picture on his Instagram with his lips locked tightly on a nurse. Chloe hadn't even troubled herself about him; she had simply smirked and turned away, ignoring him and his shenanigans. William had continued to communicate with her through texts, calls, and sometimes video. The peace-keeping mission seemed to be going well. His group's presence seemed to have quelled the previously developing problems, and he found himself with a lot of time on his hands. He had been exploring Rio de Janeiro since his arrival.

She wanted a life elsewhere, somewhere where she wouldn't think about the lack of a man in her life. Olivia had asked for a quick meeting so they could all decide where the tide would bear them this year. She parked her car and made her way into the café, her light floral dress sashaying in the hot afternoon weather. Victory Garden Café was the perfect spot for whenever they wanted to just sit and make a plan, which was why Olivia had chosen it again for this short meeting.

"Hey, hey!" Ava called out, rising out of her seat as Chloe made it over to their table.

"Hey, ladies," she called out excitedly.

"You're late!" Avery said. "I'm guessing you didn't sleep alone last night," she added.

"You guessed right; it was myself and my blanket, Avery," Chloe replied with a smile.

"If you do that for too long, something is going to get rusty," Mia quipped, prolonging the rusty and waving her hand.

"Look who's talking," Chloe said, pulling Mia into a warm embrace. "When was the last time you got that coochie worked up?"

"Last night, girl! Henri came over, and we spent all night going at it. I tell you, French men know what the tongue is built for." Mia winked. They all hooted loudly.

"American men, on the other hand, think it's designed for making fake promises," Chloe chimed in. They laughed as she pulled up a seat and slid in. "How's Antonio and Carlo?" she asked, winking at the two married members of their crew.

"My man is doing alright," Olivia said.

"Mine too," Ava quipped.

"They won't mind their women going away all summer, will they?" Avery asked.

"No, definitely not," Olivia said. "Right, Ava?" she asked.

"Yes, I'm all good to go, biiiitcheeeess!" Ava dramatized.

A waiter walked up to them at that moment bearing some croissants and coffee mugs. He laid everything out according to what the ladies had requested. When he was done, he turned to the latest member of the party and asked how she wanted her coffee. Chloe smiled, winked at him, and complimented his manners.

"Thank you. Here at Victory Garden, our customers are our number-one priority," he said.

"Good. Double mocha cappuccino, please," Chloe ordered with a smile.

"Isn't he too young?" Mia laughed as the waiter turned and

made his way back to the kitchen.

"Get your mind out of the gutter, Mia. I was only throwing him an innocent compliment," Chloe defended herself.

"Innocence doesn't look like that, Chloe," her friend accused.

"But he looks so cute. Why is he a waiter, anyway?" Chloe asked, looking a little dejected.

"Waiters are below your league, aren't they?" Olivia quipped.

"No, but that could be quite the conversation starter." Chloe replied.

"I vote Paris," Avery said, drawing everyone else's minds back to the original reason they were gathered in that café.

"Why Paris?" Mia asked.

"Chloe might find one or two decadent French boys to corrupt further, I think." Avery laughed.

"Why am I at the center of your unholy jokes this morning, ladies?" Chloe asked with mock shock written all over her face.

"Because you are displaying cougar tendencies today, baby girl. Go ahead, and talk to the delectable little waiter boy. Here he comes," Mia said giggling.

"Don't mind if I do." Chloe winked. She waited for him to arrive at their table and place the coffee and extra croissants down. He completed this with a bit of a cutesy curtsy, which intrigued Chloe even further. She looked at his name tag. "Trent" was written in bold letters across his chest. When she made to open her mouth to speak, Mia covered her face with her palm and held on until the waiter returned to his desk.

"What did you do that for?" Chloe asked.

"Oh, he's just a child. Not even eighteen. I think you need to get laid, Chloe. You'd have noticed his age if you weren't so blindly horny!" Mia quipped.

"Oh my, I nearly rapped with a minor?" Chloe asked.

"He looks horny too. You'd have had a minor for lunch," Mia said.

"Oh my God." Chloe laughed at herself. "Please, this vacation needs to happen. And by God, I need a wild one," she quipped.

"Paris is the place to be." Avery said again.

"How about Rome?" Chloe suggested.

"Weren't we just in Venice not too long ago? Come on. Someplace new will definitely do it for us all. And summer is already here. We are wasting precious daylight. If there is no other special suggestion, I vote Paris too," Ava said.

"Why is nobody mentioning the Caribbean here?" Chloe asked.

"I'm with Chloe on this one; we should probably head over there and get some sand on our asses," Olivia quipped. Chloe's phone chimed, and she picked it out of her clutch bag, drew her finger across the surface, and threw it back in.

"Who's making your cheeks rosy, Chloe?" Avery asked.

"What cheeks?" Chloe asked.

"Whoever was on the phone just made you blush crimson, and we would like to know who this person is," Avery said.

"Did she communicate her mobile number to the waiter boy through some kind of telepathy?" Mia asked.

"You all better stop this thing," Chloe enjoined.

"Spill, babe. We want to know who the mystery man is," Olivia said. They all leaned their arms on the table and bored their eyes into hers.

"Okay, okay, it's William. You remember William?" she asked.

"Soldier boy?" they chorused.

"He's a man," she pouted.

"Oh, honey, we know," Olivia said.

"He is much older than the waiter boy," she continued.

"Of course," Avery chimed in. Chloe's phone rang out loud this time, and she grabbed it and stared at the screen.

"What's the problem, Chloe? Why don't you want to pick up?" Mia asked.

"He's calling on video," Chloe said.

"We will be extremely quiet," Olivia said, looking around the table to get the consent of the other ladies. Chloe looked at them a moment before pressing the button to initiate the call.

"Hi, Will," she said.

"Oooohhh," the ladies chorused.

"You guys promised!" Chloe chided.

"Who are you with?" The male voice came wafting through.

"My friends," Chloe replied.

"Hi, Will," all of them chorused to Chloe's chagrin.

"Can you turn the camera around, Chloe? Just let me say a quick hello?" he asked. Chloe switched to her phone's rear camera while staring daggers at her friends.

"Hi, ladies," he said, waving at them with a big smile playing across his face. "How are you all doing?" he asked.

"We're doing pretty good," they chorused.

"Okay, that's enough," Chloe said, reverting the camera back to herself. "Hey, Will, how's it going with you?" she asked.

"The sun is just wasting away over here. I was wondering if you already had summer plans?" he asked with a hopeful look in his eyes.

"Well, I do have . . ." Chloe began.

"Can we come too?" Olivia asked, rushing over to appear in the video call with the other ladies following suit. "I promise you guys won't even know we are there. I promise we will be almost invisible," Olivia quipped.

"There is no . . ." Chloe began again.

"We are actually here trying to brainstorm the best spot for a summer holiday. Where are you at again? She told us once, but I don't remember what she said exactly," Avery said.

"Sunny Rio de Janeiro. You guys are going to love everything about this place. You should definitely come down here and have yourselves a summer to remember," William advised.

"Oh my world!" Mia cooed. "Why didn't we think of South America in all our plans?" she asked.

"That's true! South America is actually great this time of year. We will definitely enjoy everything it offers," Olivia said, pinching Chloe, who jumped slightly.

"What do you say, Chloe?" William asked. All of their eyes reverted back to her, and they all waited for her response to this new proposition. She didn't say a word. For the next few minutes, all Chloe wanted to do was run away from her friends to the comfort of her bed and the safety of her apartment. But all their eyes were on her, and she couldn't just stand and run away from them. Instead she stared at William and the waterfront on which he seemed to be standing. His call from the beachfront made it seem like he perfectly planned all of this. The only part he wouldn't have been able to predict was that she would be with her ladies at this time. It had helped tremendously. She would have been able to say no if she were home, but here, she almost had no option.

"Alright, I guess it wouldn't hurt," she said. Her ladies hooted and jumped excitedly. Olivia wrapped her hand around Chloe's neck and held tight for a moment. "You lot are very bad friends," Chloe said.

"No matter how you feel about him, you just took one for the team, and we will always remember that." Ava laughed.

Chloe went back to her apartment, worried, her thoughts constantly returning to William and how similar he was to Francis. She didn't leave one emotionally unavailable man to jump into the arms of another. She was willing to admit that William was more emotionally available than Francis would ever be, but the similitudes were just too much to be ignored.

She would flow with the tide, and she was thankful that the motion of the tide was slow and gentle. She hoped that meant she would easily jump off at any point when she felt the water was no longer a comfortable place for her to be. She would keep an eye out and watch for the right time to make a decision that would save her from a long and tumultuous emotional rollercoaster.

She slept that night with the waters of Prainha in her mind. It wouldn't be a bad summer after all; she was sure of that. If there was nothing else to enjoy, she would have as much fun as possible enjoying the view of the waters and the scenery. She picked up her phone and went online. If she was headed to Rio, she might as well make sure she knew where all the best things were so she didn't end up missing anything.

CHAPTER 4

When the sun prepared to make its way daintily across the face of the sky, chasing the darkness off into small pockets in corners not visible to the eyes, William rose from his bed and stretched quickly. He made his way into the bathroom to brush his teeth and wash off the remnants of the night from his face. Last night had been the only night since his group's arrival where there was even the slightest contact between them and the band of miscreants trying to sneak into South America.

Terrorism had never been a real problem in these parts. It had always been in the Middle East and Europe; even Africa had seen more terrorist attacks than this place. Here, though, it was now rearing its ugly head like it had done in other parts of the world. The bombing of the Argentine Israelite Mutual Association building in Buenos Aires, Argentina, had killed about eighty-five people and injured ten times more than that. But there was little of that reported in Brazil in the past few years. There were just a few reports here and there, but no mass-casualty events. And no one certainly ever heard of a band of radical Islamists cooking up plans to stay in the mountains of Rio de Janeiro and wreak havoc on the surrounding valleys.

He stepped out of the bath and wiped his face with a towel before falling to the floor for his routine of early morning pushups. When he was done, he rose off the floor, dressed in his camos, and put on his boots and backpack. He always went on early morning runs, lugging his backpack on his back. His commander didn't mind; he let him do whatever he wanted in order to keep himself in tip-top shape.

The men were already gathered, going through some routine stretching exercises. One of them had been hit last night in the short shoot-out with the terrorists. Everyone's faces were slightly somber; suddenly everything had become real for them, and not just the tame assignment it had been for the past two months since they had arrived. William's team leader, Sergeant Major Kevin McCaw, was on the phone when he walked up. He waited, his hands to his sides as he listened to the conversation without listening to it.

"Sergeant Hanley, you lead these men on the run this morning. I have a meeting to attend right away," he said and turned away, making his way off to the quarters. They had been living there, in the officer's mess of the embassy building. William turned to the men and appraised them quickly, making sure their somberness hadn't rendered them complacent.

"Form up on me!" he called out.

They formed a perfect square with him as the spearhead, and off they went. The streets of Rio were quiet at this hour. The sun was sailing across the sky, its face hidden beneath the clouds, its orange glow seeping through the whiteness that pervaded the sky. William didn't notice it. Instead, his thoughts went back to the night before. They had not been expecting trouble. It was almost like they had let their guards down because they hadn't encountered any trouble since their arrival. And so they made the worst mistake a soldier at war could: complacency.

They had been sitting outside, enjoying the coolness of the evening, when Kenny Hawthorne suggested they step outdoors and see what nightlife they could rustle up around there. They had stepped out, leaving their weapons behind. They didn't think they would need them. After all, they were only looking to have themselves some good old innocent fun.

They hadn't walked very far from the embassy building when a dark sedan pulled out quickly in front of them and a head poked out of the car window. The sounds of gunshots then pervaded the hitherto quiet night. He could remember every bit of that event like it was burned into his frontal lobe. His reaction had been one of the reasons more of the men weren't hurt. The sight of the car pulling out in front of them had thrown him into quick action, and he had yelled for the men to take cover. The others dove to the ground quickly. A bullet had grazed William's arm, but he had managed to drag himself out of the line of fire and stayed down until the salvo of bullets ceased, which lasted only a few minutes and ended with the sedan driving off. William later wondered why they hadn't gotten out of the car to finish them off considering none of his company had returned fire because none of them was packing any heat.

He thought about that as they worked to stop the bleeding on Kenny's arm and as they carried him to the embassy hospital. He also thought of their complacency that almost had them killed. They should at least have had sidearms with them; that was standard in places like this with such threats roaming the streets. You were never overprepared with a sidearm tucked into your pants.

They now ran up the Santa Luiz, pacing themselves as they went. He patted the side of his belt that held his sidearm, making sure he would not be surprised again. As they ran, his eyes caught two lovers making their way from the beach early in the morning. Holiday makers were already here, and these two had probably spent all night on the beach, enjoying the sight of the stars that dotted the night sky. Watching them trudge home under the light of the sun reminded him that a lot of tourists would be down here soon. This little unrest wouldn't stop a lot of them from trooping in, and his team would likely be responsible for a lot of these clueless tourists.

His mind went to Chloe, and a smile broke out across his face. Just as fast as the smile had appeared, it disappeared, leaving him with worry as he began to imagine her here in the madness of Rio. Maybe he had been in too much of a hurry to bring her over. Maybe he shouldn't have suggested she come over here with her friends.

What's worse was the fact that she hadn't even wanted to come over here. He had made her, almost ambushing her and riding on the coattails of her friends to make it possible. A dangerous place like this was not the best spot for a vacation, and he was only realizing that at this moment.

His brow wrinkled with worry, and he found himself growing even more worried the more he thought about it. He shrugged it off and ran, forgetting the worry like the backpack on his back. They made the return lap, keeping the run to an hour in all.

"A penny for your thoughts, Sarge?" Henry Jameson asked, running up beside William. They had been tight since their first mission down in Madrid. It was the first time this team had come together. He had been brought into this new team to provide sniper support, and he had felt like an alien amongst these men until Jameson helped him feel like a real member of the team.

"That's a cheap price to pay for my thoughts, son, so make it a reasonable price for me," William replied.

"I could get any woman out of Rio for you. You've just got to want to be involved with her," Henry quipped.

"You're going to get winded if you keep talking so much, Henry," William chided. Henry pulled back a little and fell into line, laughing out loud as William dodged yet another attempt to put him together with a woman. In the early days, he had thought the man was some kind of celibate with his rejections to the thing most men rush at. He later learned that he had been burned one too many times and preferred to stay away from love. It had been surprising to hear of his chance encounter with a woman that had become so engrained into his memory that he had planned extensively to go to her in New York when his leave came knocking. It hadn't gone so well for him, and Henry felt saddened by the fact that William hadn't gotten what he wanted out of it.

As they made their way back to the embassy, Sergeant Major McCaw was standing outside the building with a woman William had never met before. This woman was tall and had blue eyes that seemed to pierce right through one's soul. He stared as they approached, wondering what she was doing there with the major at that moment.

It was not that he hadn't worked with women who were excellent soldiers. Halsey was a woman, and she was no less of a member of the team. But this woman felt different, and he couldn't tell how; it slightly freaked him out. As the men lined up to listen to the team leader, William walked up to stand beside him as the assistant team leader. Things might be escalating, and he would like to know who this lady was and what she would bring to their group.

"Gentlemen, this is Gertrude Winter. She is going to be our resident shrink, sorry, psychologist," he said. The men chuckled at the mistake from the captain. William expected Gertrude to react, but she only smiled and took the stage at McCaw's prompting.

"I know you don't really have a need for a psychologist out here in the middle of nowhere. As a matter of fact, I know you don't need a psychologist at all, but here's what we are going to do: You try and see me once every month, and I will pretend you still don't need me!" She smiled a contagious smile that rested delicately on the corners of her upper lip. "Gentlemen, these weekly check-in meetings are nonnegotiable, especially if you want to remain a soldier in this man's army," she said.

"Umm, ma'am, why now?" a voice called out of the group of ten men.

"Uncle Sam finally thinks his soldiers deserve to have a normal and good life, and it is my job to make sure you get all that he is offering you." she said. "Any further questions?"

There was silence, and McCaw was quick to thank her and advise the men to make sure they visit the good doctor to ensure that they remain a part of this team. Dismissed, they all ambled off toward their quarters. As William made his way off, Gertrude called out to him.

"Hi," she said, stretching her hand out to him. "Gertrude Winter. You are Sergeant William Hanley?" she asked.

"Yes, nice to make your acquaintance," he replied.

"Yes, I feel the same. You mind telling me what you were doing out there with your men at night when they ought to have been in bed or at most within the embassy building considering what has been going on out there?" she asked.

"Excuse me?" he asked incredulously.

"You were the most senior officer on the team that night, and you got one of your men shot because you cared more about having fun than you did about your soldiers," she said.

"You're making this into some kind of blame-throwing bit where I'm thrown under the bus for being shot at." he defended.

"I would love to talk more about this with you later. I have scheduled a session with you tomorrow. Be sure to come to my office, alright?" she said.

William turned away and walked off, never looking back as he made his way back to the quarters. He couldn't fathom how she could jump to conclusions like that without thinking about it first. He had been with the men when the unfortunate incident took place, but he hadn't pushed them in front of danger. It hadn't been his suggestion in the first place, and when he felt the avalanche falling, he had tried his best to defend his men.

Henry walked into the room and sat beside him on the bed, watching his face as it still took in the myriad of information that assailed him. He could hear it now, the argument where he was guilty of leading his men into trouble. If he hadn't agreed to the stupid outing that night, they wouldn't have gone. It was that simple, yet he couldn't help but think the accusation a little harsh on himself.

"She's a pretty little dish, isn't she?" Henry asked as he came in after William.

"Oh come on. She's a blonde and probably doesn't know what's what," William said.

"Is she a psychologist or a psychiatrist? Whichever one she is, she is probably going to be a smart woman, don't you think?" he asked.

"I don't really care, Henry." William said, pulling off his boots and sliding them into the corner. He then pulled off his pants and walked into the bathroom while Henry stood outside talking about Gertrude's skin, her smile, and the delicate nature of her mien.

"She's a man-eater, Henry. You both probably deserve each other," William said as he stepped out of the bathroom with a towel wrapped about his waist. His taut torso and prominent muscles made his body a sight to behold.

"You think so?" Henry asked.

"If you don't get out of here right away, I promise you I'll force my foot on a delicate part of your body!" William said.

"All problems are not to be solved through violence, William," Henry said as he ambled away.

"Don't I know that?" he called after him, throwing off the towel.

CHAPTER 5

Chloe had never been one to overthink or second-guess herself, but this trip to Rio was beginning to feel like a chore to her. She would simply pull out if she could, but her ladies were all too excited, and she couldn't renege on them at this point.

William was an appealing man. She had enjoyed his mannerisms at the airport when he had bumped into her and a few months back when he had visited New York on vacation. He was the ideal man, one with delicate tastes. His choice of a restaurant for that little date had been terrific. She would love to head back there and enjoy the beef made by Chef Montes. But she was scared. She knew what proximity did to her and how she might feel swept off her feet until the ghosting and the missions came, leaving her alone once more with a man who was never around. She couldn't do that to herself again, yet she couldn't wiggle her way out of this vacation.

A thought ran through her like pieces of debris floating on the surface of the ocean. There was nothing in William's behavior to indicate that he might like or want her. Instead, he had been acting just like any other man. He had suggested they come down to Rio. There was never any time in the course of the conversation where he had mentioned that he would pay for them to come over. That would have sent some kind of concrete sign of his affection. It wasn't about the money. It was more about the gesture, which would speak more strongly of how much he wanted her over there.

During that night they had spent in New York together, he hadn't said anything, maybe because their time together was brief. He had left the next day and probably had no time to say what was really on his mind. But even now, Chloe, who had spent a lot of time working with people and could read them with such ease, could feel that he wasn't just in New York on vacation. A couple of things pointed to that theory.

He had come down to her show and had sought her out afterward to fix a date. He had hoped to have more time in New York, but that didn't end up happening, and therein lay her second suspicion. She had seen him look down at his beeper when it went off. The disappointment on his face was very clear for anyone looking to see. He hadn't wanted to leave, and she could tell.

Their trip was to begin the next day, and even now she was still unsure of whether or not she wanted to be down there with William. The city itself was not the problem. She had heard wonderful things about Rio, and she was in no doubt that they would have so much fun down there. Her worries came from another angle. She didn't know what she was walking into, and that troubled her. She opened her Louis Vuitton bag and began placing some clothes into it. She had everything she would need on the bed as she always did before a trip. First, she laid them all out and took them in with her eyes, making sure she hadn't forgotten anything.

She began to throw them into her bag, picking them up one after the other when her doorbell chimed. She walked to the window to see who was at the door. A big smile broke out on her face as she caught sight of the ladies standing outside.

"You all look too ready for this vacation!" she cooed as she opened the door to let them in, throwing her arms open to welcome them. As always, they fell into each other's arms, holding tight for a moment as wide smiles covered their faces. They lugged their bags into the apartment. She stared at the bags with a bit of envy running through her mind. She wished she had finished her packing and was all ready to head off to Rio.

"I'm guessing you haven't packed anything yet, Chloe?" Mia said, staring into her eyes.

"Well, I've started," she said, smiling to cover the fact that once again, she was the last to pack her things, except for that one time when Olivia was the last to pack because she didn't know about the vacation.

"Tell me you at least booked the flight with the airline?" Olivia quipped.

"Oh my God!" she exclaimed, running to her phone. She grabbed the phone and pulled it up to her ear.

"Are you sure we can still get something good at this hour?" Avery asked.

"I'm sorry, it completely escaped my mind. I'll see what they have. You lot aren't angry at me, are you?" She apologized. A sensuous, deep baritone came over the line, and she smiled as she said a quick hello.

"May I get five tickets to Rio for tomorrow?" she asked.

"Five?" the voice asked, trying to confirm what she had said.

"Yes please," she said.

"Sure, I think we can fix you in on the 3:00 p.m. flight to Rio. Can you give me the names for the tickets?" the voice asked.

"Chloe Baxter, Olivia Sullivan, Ava Hogan . . . "

"Wait, these names have already been booked with us for a trip to Rio. It's only the time I need to confirm," he said.

"Give me a minute, and I'll call you back," Chloe said, turning to her friends with mock anger on her face.

"Which of you sneaky girls booked the flight and sat there watching me make a fool of myself?" she asked, her eyes boring into her friends.

"I sure didn't do it," Olivia said, turning to Avery.

"Me either," rang out among the ladies, and they all had genuine surprise in their eyes as they all said no to the ticket issue. She didn't want it to be true. There was only one person left that could have done this. Thinking about it, she was sure he had done it. There was no other explanation. He had asked a few days earlier which ladies had agreed to head off to Rio. She had told him they would book a flight at JFK without thinking that he would go ahead and make the payment for their tickets. She called the airline back and got the same guy on the line.

"Hi. It's me again. What time is our flight tomorrow?" she asked.

"It's 10:00 a.m., ma'am," the customer-service guy replied.

"Could you tell me who paid for the tickets?" she asked.

"A Sergeant Hanley paid for the tickets," he replied.

"Alright, thank you very much," she said and ended the call.

"What's going on, Chloe?" Olivia asked.

"William already paid for our tickets. All we have to do is get on the plane and head on down to Rio," she said.

"Oh wow, he must really like you," Mia said.

"He must really want her down there with him," Avery chipped in.

"There's that too!" Ava quipped.

"Oh wow, are we witnessing love budding?" Olivia asked, stepping in and wrapping her hands around Chloe, smiling into her face. Chloe didn't know what to think. She worried that he was doing too much for some feelings she wasn't sure she could reciprocate.

"You lot are always seeing something where there's nothing. I'm not interested in William in that way. We're just friends," Chloe said.

"Said every girl right before she fell head over heels in love with the man of her dreams," Olivia said.

"Liv, I'm serious. There's nothing. Not now. Not before. We don't even know each other that well," Chloe said.

"Well, there's only one thing that will settle this," Mia said.

"What's that?" Chloe asked.

"A pros-and-cons list. I'm sure that's what you're already doing in your mind. You want to know whether you should at least give it a try. And right now, you don't have the full picture because everything appears fragmented." Mia explained.

"Oh, please, no. He's just like Francis: never around. I'm not going to do that to myself again," Chloe said and turned, making her way back into her bedroom to continue with her packing. They watched her leave, each of them holding their own thoughts in their minds. They were on the same wavelength, and if they knew how identical their thoughts were at that moment, they would laugh so hard their bellies would ache. They all thought she would succumb. They would also agree that William was a big gesture guy and no woman had ever been able to resist the big gestures. They walked into the bedroom and found Chloe picking up her clothes and folding them gently into her bag.

"Mia, how did you conclude that little kerfuffle with your man?" Chloe asked.

"Well, let's just say I'm heading into this vacation single. I'm all ready to hop on a good old train and pull on the cord to make sure the bells ring!" she said with a big smile on her face.

"Oh, honey, what happened?" Olivia moved closer with the others leaving what they were doing to draw closer to their friend. She had been dating a finance guy for the past year or more. She had been threatening to leave him for a while, but this was the first time she was saying it was over. There was nothing to say. She had made her decision, and they all supported her. It was always best to walk away when you didn't see any kind of future with the man you were with.

"Come on, this isn't an occasion for sadness. He's not worth it. Just imagine me and some of those half-dressed beach boys down in the heart of Christ country. Imagine me kissing a pretty little man with Christ the Redeemer watching on and nodding his support," she said bursting into laughter.

"The Christians will dig into you if they hear that blasphemy coming from your mouth," Chloe chided.

"Well, there ain't no Christians in this room, are there? Because Christ might see more than that when I get on them beaches. I plan on getting some sand in this pussy," she said, pointing down at her crotch.

"Damn girl, you're just nasty!" Avery laughed. Chloe slapped Mia's ass and pushed her shoulder.

"Too bad for the married hotties in this group. We can get sand in it all right, but we can't get it out until we get back to our men who are apparently too busy to come with us," Olivia said.

"Your loss. No one asked you lot to go get married," Chloe quipped, chuckling. Olivia and Ava shook their heads as they shared a look. They would have to content themselves with fun that was within the boundaries and not go all gung ho like they would have done when they were single. This time, it would be all tame and PG-13.

"Here's an idea," Chloe said, turning to Ava and Olivia. "When the two of you want to forget you're married, just give me your rings to hold on to for you guys. You can go crazy when I take them rings away from your hands." She chuckled.

"You're evil, Chloe," Olivia said.

"Thank you! If I don't help you, who will?" she replied.

CHAPTER 6

Their Ubers were waiting downstairs at nine o'clock in the morning. It would take them about thirty minutes to get to JFK. When they walked out of the house, the excitement was playing like a stroboscope right on their faces. It was loud and overt. They were so happy to head out of New York for the summer. They wore light dresses that billowed in the light as they sashayed to the vehicles. Olivia, Chloe, and Mia got into one Uber, while the others got into the other.

"We should have made this transport one for the married and the other for the singles because you know how it is," Mia said.

"Liv, what do you have to say for yourself? Are you going to bore us with husband talk?" Chloe asked.

"You're both crazy. When have I ever bored you with husband talk?" she asked incredulously.

"We're not saying you have. We're only saying what we have seen many married women do in public: they bore the crap out of everybody," Chloe said bursting into loud laughter harmonized by Mia's deep, throaty appeal.

"You lot are just bonkers," Liv said.

They made good time. New York traffic was surprisingly mild at this hour, and the drivers were able to get them to JFK in less than thirty minutes. They stepped out of the vehicles and made their way into the lobby and on to the waiting area. Chloe went with Olivia to pick up their tickets. Liv had been looking for a chance to speak with Chloe alone.

"Chloe, baby, you know this William man likes you," she began.

"Yeah, it looks that way, but I'm sure I don't want the Francis dynamics all over again. That shit drained me. I'm grateful he gave me a good reason to walk away, otherwise I'd be out there waiting while he was off somewhere locking lips with one of his fat nurse friends," Chloe replied.

"Oh, you suspected he was cheating?" Olivia asked.

"In retrospect, I guess. He wouldn't call for a long time, and when he eventually did, there was always a female voice around. I chalked all that up to the fact that he had to work with a lot of people and half the time he was with people. I actually felt important when he called me with people around. Little did I know. Of course, I might be wrong, but you can see why I don't want to have anything to do with a man who's thrown into the deep end most of the time, right?" Chloe asked.

"Yes, I do." she replied. They were now at the counter, which temporarily quelled their conversation. Chloe spoke to the receptionist, who picked out their tickets and handed them over. When they turned around and made their way back to the others, Olivia couldn't hold in her thoughts any longer.

"I'm sorry Francis turned out to be a capital douche. The problem with bastards like him is that they make you feel so bad, so low, that you can't look past them to see what's staring you right in the face. That sort of vision, the type that keeps our eyes on those who have hurt us the most, is the worst type of vision to have," she advised.

"You think I should give William a chance?" she asked.

"I do," Olivia replied.

"I don't know, Liv. I keep thinking about it, and each time, I have Francis's useless face laughing hysterically in mine. Most times I just want to grab his beard and pull it out at the same time," she said.

"Does he have a beard?" Olivia asked.

"He lets it grow when he's out on missions. One time, he said the local women love a man with a beard, and I didn't think anything of it," she said.

"Jeez!" Olivia exclaimed.

"I've never felt so much like a fool in all my life. I kept asking myself if I was in some kind of daze or hallucinating or something because what the fuck happened to me?" Chloe asked.

"You liked him; that's just what it is. I'm happy you broke free of him. Now you must work to gain full victory, which only comes if you don't let him dictate all your moves. Actually, he shouldn't dictate any of your moves at all," she said.

"He shouldn't have any power over me at all," Chloe agreed, but she knew even as the words left her mouth that she wasn't going to keep to them as she should. Olivia had a point, and she could see it. Giving that bastard more power to decide her next moves for her only set her up for more pain. If she refused to give life and love a chance because she had been hurt in the past, she would continue hurting long after the one who hurt her had moved on.

"Took you guys long enough. We were beginning to think you met some cute boys out there and decided to get nasty before Rio, which would have been awesome except that we then realized that Chloe had gone off with a married woman, which officially dropped the awesome level down a notch." Mia laughed. Olivia chased her, ready to smack her bum right there for her constant teasing.

"Mia, if you don't get a man in fucking Rio, I will never forgive you!" Ava said with mock seriousness, grabbing her bags and moving forward as the first onboarding calls were made. They should have been waiting in the first-class lounge since they arrived, but they didn't know William had booked first-class tickets until they picked them up. It was already time to board the aircraft by the time they found this out. They trooped in with wide smiles dotting their faces. Mia was practically whistling as she made her way into the plane, and the others laughed at her mannerisms. She had always been like this: carefree and sometimes a little weird.

She had grown up in a Texas, and while she had lost the Texan tongue somewhere along the line, she could still whip it out when she needed to go ballistic on someone. She was the calmest of all of them. She spoke softly and carried herself with a certain grace most of the time except for moments when she was provoked emotionally. In this particular moment, happiness had re-awakened the Texan in her, which was why she was whistling and dancing a little on her feet as she made her way into the airplane. She did the same when she got angry: she would launch into her Texan alter ego and tear the whole place up both literally and figuratively.

Chloe smiled, watching Mia's happiness as they embarked. They stowed their bags away and took their seats. There were plates of fruit littering the first-class aisle, and they picked some up as they made their way to their seats. William had picked some excellent seats where they could all sit together for the flight. He had been very thoughtful with every part of this arrangement, which made Chloe smile further.

"He went all out here, didn't he?" Olivia asked.

"Yeah, he did," Chloe said with starry eyes.

They strapped in, sitting pert as the aircraft lifted off the ground. This was always the most terrifying part of the trip for Avery, who didn't like flying very much. She held her breath, stiffened her limbs, and closed her eyes as the plane taxied on the runway. Chloe placed a gentle palm on her lap, holding her down and whispering to her just to let her know that she wasn't alone.

***

A statue of Christ the Redeemer loomed large on the horizon as they began their descent into Rio de Janeiro. Its arms were stretched, open to those who came into the blissful city. It reminded Chloe of the Statue of Liberty, the colossus standing tall in New York with the poetry of Emma Lazarus bedecking it. She felt welcome, almost like someone had invited her. She smiled, her eyes taking in the whole vista.

For the first time in a long time, she prayed. There were no words, and nothing was said except for a deep yearning in her heart, but she hoped that Christ would see through her and proffer answers to her prayers and desires. The waters were visible from up there; they were blue, with roads snaking around them, winding to and away from them. She saw what had to be Copacabana, which had popped up a lot when she searched for some of the best things to do in Rio. The sandy beaches beckoned, and she smiled, happy that she had answered. She should probably say her thanks to William when she saw him. He had gone to great lengths to make sure that she came to enjoy this beautiful city and its captivating vistas.

The urban jungles with mountain peaks scattered within stared up at their aircraft as they flew closer. Chloe couldn't keep her eyes off the beauty of the terrain. There was a bit of it that seemed to have been arranged by the invisible hands of a being whose power was unrivaled. It was why the whole landscape looked like a piece of art, painted by the hands of a skilled artist. As the aircraft drew lower, the vista disappeared, and the more urban parts of the city presented itself. The high-rise buildings dotting the heart of Rio came rushing up at them, tall, ordered, and juxtaposed against the statue of Christ the Redeemer, who seemed to be staring down at the city, watching over it as it welcomed newcomers.

When the plane taxied to a stop, they stepped out with smiles on their faces. None of them had been there before, but they were never worried about navigating the city and getting around. Most times, all you had to do was ask, and there would be a transport system there to take you wherever you would like to go.

"Is this beautiful or what?" Olivia asked as they stepped into the exterior of the Galeao International Airport.

"How is this any better than what we're used to in other countries and airports?" Avery asked.

"Now she speaks!" Chloe laughed.

"Of course I speak. When the solid earth is right under my feet, I speak, and I speak out loud," She laughed.

"Don't go getting on Liv's nerves now. If she says the airport is the most beautiful she has ever seen, then it must be true." Chloe laughed. The ladies all broke into laughter, and Olivia chased after Chloe. It was surprising to Mia how the two of them were able to run in their high-heeled shoes with such ease. Olivia caught up and gave Chloe a light tap on her bum.

The Galeao was bland, with no greenery around at all. They

must have thought that Rio de Janeiro already had too many forests to even have a bit of grass at the Galeao Airport. The architecture was quite impressive, though, and that might really be what Olivia was referring to when she spoke of the beauty of the place.

"Is it the architecture that pleases you?" Mia asked.

"No, more like the novelty of it all. It's all so new that I have no choice but to like this place." she explained.

When they walked into the lobby, they all had to rethink their position on the appeal of the airport. While it looked old and ill maintained, the feeling of being within an antique place pervaded them. And Olivia with her imaginative eyes could already see what the outcome would be if the original whiteness of the walls had a new coat of paint.

Chloe was beginning to wonder why they had to land there. They could have landed elsewhere, a much more appealing airport. The biggest appeal of this airport was its proximity to the city and the sight as you entered. It was quite breathtaking, and Chloe wasn't sure she would ever forget what she felt at the sight of that vista. It had done something to her mind.

"Chloe," Olivia called.

"What is it?" she asked, turning around.

"Isn't that your man?" Olivia asked.

"Which man? Francis?" Chloe asked, turning around quickly.

"Is there a human named Francis in this universe?" Olivia asked.

"Oh, William? Is he here?" Chloe asked. Her eyes caught him at that moment, clad in army slacks and a green T-shirt tucked into his pants. He held a placard over his head with a sweet smile on his face. She admired his manliness, a small smile breaking out on her face too as she watched him. She didn't know that she blushed crimson at the sight of the well-built William and his disarming smile.

"Umm, Chloe, what's the situation between you too again? Is he fair game? Can I get in there and see what we can talk about? What do you think?" Avery asked, her eyes riveted on the man. She waved lightly, as did most of the girls.

"Avery, you'll find a good man that will take care of you, but take your eyes off of William," Chloe said.

"But you don't want him, do you? Look at those abs inside that shirt. Just imagine what happens when he takes off those clothes and presents the whole thing as an exhibition for you alone," Avery continued.

"Oh my God, Avery!" Mia's eyes widened in surprise.

"That's not a bad picture though," Olivia said.

"You're married, aren't you, Liv?" Chloe asked.

"Nobody ever said we shouldn't look around at God's perfect handiwork." Olivia said.

"Adultery much?" Mia said.

"We should walk over to him. We look like the cast of a silly movie standing here and watching him," Ava said. They started walking down upon hearing Ava's words. It was almost like a pre-planned scene as they walked in tandem, beautiful, elegant with their steps almost in synchrony with each other.

"I can't be part of a cast of a stupid movie," Chloe said, turning to cast her eyes on Ava.

"Well, if you had stood there any longer, you would have been the lead character in a stupid movie," Ava quipped, and they all burst into laughter, grabbing their stomachs at the banal conversation.

"Hello, ladies!" William called out as they drew closer. "You guys seem to be having fun already," he said with a smile on his face.

"You could have walked up to us, you know?" Chloe said.

"Chloe! Give the man some credit!" Olivia chided.

"Actually I would have except that I saw you guys enjoying yourselves, and I figured I had best leave you to it." He smiled.

"Thank you for coming, William," Chloe said, smiling.

"You're . . . " William began.

"William! I've been waiting out here for almost an hour. If the flight is delayed, then we've got to head back to the embassy," a sweet-sounding feminine voice called out. They all turned around immediately and stared at the new entrant as she walked into the room. She was a tall, pretty blonde woman in a uniform. She was so pretty that for a moment, the ladies were at a loss for words.

There was silence, and this lady and the others just stared at each other.

"Oh, ladies, this is Gertrude Winter. Gertrude, this is Chloe, Olivia, Ava, Mia, and Avery," William introduced quickly, his hand going over them all as he made the quick introduction.

"Hello," Olivia said, extending her hand out. Gertrude shook the hand, smiling pleasantly. She looked even prettier when she smiled. She shook hands with everyone. Chloe gave her a limp handshake before they all walked out of the airport lobby and made their way out into the open after William, who led them to two cars waiting outside. He spoke to the drivers of the cars, got back in the embassy vehicle with Gertrude, and drove ahead with the other car bringing up the rear.

It took them over thirty minutes to get to the hotel. Chloe was quiet throughout the ride; her eyes were glued to car window, staring out at the traffic and the pedestrians walking the streets. She saw some holiday makers who looked just as excited as her ladies in the vehicle did. She didn't want to think about the woman with William in the vehicle. She looked like she was in the military too, and she couldn't blame him for bringing a colleague along.

She didn't want to think about any of it. She only wanted to concentrate on getting to the hotel and resting her head for a second. Yet all she could think of was the woman with William in the car and what they might be talking about. Gertrude could have her lips locked with his in a tight kiss at that moment for all she knew. She didn't blame him. She had been the one yelling about how she wanted to keep everything casual, yet she was the one worrying about the woman with whom he was spending his time with.

The sight of Copacabana Beach with its blue waters and beautiful expanse captivated the ladies as the driver drove them to their hotel. They watched some holiday makers on the beach, enjoying their day with some sporting activities. The beach volleyball caught Chloe's eye, and she watched some of the handsome young men bouncing around in the water. There were women sunbathing in bikinis while a few kids ran along the shore, and other children held adult hands in their tiny fingers.

"Are you doing okay, Chloe?" Olivia asked as their car drove along the beach.

"Yes, yes, I'm alright. But a hotel bed can't come quick enough right now," she said. The sight of the hotel piqued her waning interest, and she sat up. Olivia had turned her face away too; she probably hadn't heard Chloe's answer to her own question. They were taken in by the elegance of Copacabana Palace. For a few minutes, they were all silent, their words swallowed up completely by the beauty of the place. It was Olivia who broke the silence; she cooed loudly, and the others quickly found their voices too.

"This is the hotel to swallow all other hotels!" Avery said, her eyes wide. They stepped out of the car. None of them could easily think of another hotel more elegant than the beauty they were currently staring at. William was standing with his back against the car, waiting for the awestruck ladies to come down from their elevated states.

The building itself was a well-crafted piece of art. It looked every bit as artsy as it was exquisitely beautiful. The hotel design was a throwback to some of the biggest hotels of the nineteenth century, with the architectural pattern a tribute to the excellence of times gone by. The compound itself appeared endless, with two major buildings within. The ornate white building looked like a colossus, and they stared at its peak as it extended into the skyline.

"Liv, are you seeing this?" Ava asked, getting out of the car with Mia in tow.

"This is crazy beautiful," she said as they made their way into the lobby. The beauty on the outside was nothing to be compared with the quaint interior decked out in appealing retro pieces of artsy furniture. Whichever way their eyes fell, they found beauty scattered everywhere. From the chairs to the pieces of art hanging on the walls, everything looked beautiful.

"Did you pick out this place yourself?" Olivia asked, her eyes still taking in the magnificence all around them.

"Yes," William answered. "We had a short stint around here in the early days of our mission. We got some reports that some of the undesirables we were looking for were hiding out here at Copacabana Beach, so we hastened after them. Turns out, terrorists aren't really interested in being caught sunning themselves at the beach without their firearms beside them," he joked.

"What made you think we would like it?" Mia chipped in.

"Chloe always looked like the artsy type, and besides, a model who's organized shows all over would probably know a thing or two about lodging and that kind of stuff. I wasn't going to put her up in some subpar place. Are you okay, Chloe?" he asked, noticing how quiet she had become.

"Oh yes, I'm okay. The beauty in here has me in a choke hold," she said.

"I'm glad you like it," he said. "A lot of celebrities have lodged in this hotel through the years, and that has made some of the rooms a lot more desirable. The room I got you guys was once occupied by the Rolling Stones. Can you believe that? It sounds crazy, but it's the truth." he said.

"Damn! The history here isn't just in the building and the exquisite beauty of the place but also in the legendary people who have stayed within these doors." Ava quipped.

"What does it matter who has lain in the bed? Unless they left some money in there before they left, I don't really care who lay in the bed and who didn't." Mia said.

They took a bit of time exploring the ground floor of the hotel before the concierge bore their luggage up to the fourth floor. William left them at that time, apologizing that he wouldn't be able to stay to see them settle in.

"We have a little assignment to handle over in Sao Paulo. I had to beg Gertrude to give me an hour for a little detour so I could get you guys out here before we continue our trip," he said, his eyes pleading for understanding even as he spoke.

"That's okay, William. We can't thank you enough for all you've done for us," Olivia said, noticing that Chloe wasn't in the mood to talk. He turned and made his way out, then almost like he forgot something, he returned quickly.

"Chloe, can I pick you up tomorrow evening? I know you would like to rest and get the long journey out of your system, but I would love to spend some time with you," he said.

"Umm, I . . . " Chloe began.

"Of course you can pick her up tomorrow. Just call before you head out so she won't be keeping you waiting," Olivia chimed in.

"I'm sorry, ladies. I have some real ass tours planned for you guys, but this little thing tomorrow is just a little something for Chloe and me to get reacquainted. I hope you all understand?" William pleaded.

"It's okay, William. We get it," Ava answered this time. He turned around, rubbed his palms as he walked out of the lobby, and made his way outside. Chloe watched him leave, giving herself a mental slap as she watched him step out into the open air.

The concierge put the luggage in their room and stood waiting for his tip. Olivia took care of it and walked back into the room.

"What's going on, Chloe? You haven't been yourself since the airport. Is everything okay?" Olivia asked.

"How can you ask that? Did you not see that pretty blonde damsel that came with Prince Charming?" Ava asked.

"She might just be a coworker or something," Mia said.

"Did you see the uniform on her? The way she was dressed was bound to make a man's eyes turn," Ava stated.

"Not helpful, Ava" Olivia said.

"We could've asked who she was or what she was doing at the airport with him," Mia stated.

"Didn't he say they were going to Sao Paulo and only took a detour?" Olivia asked. "Chloe, come on, he wouldn't be doing all of this if he didn't like you," Olivia said.

"Didn't you say you don't know if you two could be a thing?" Mia said.

"Not helping, Mia!" Olivia quipped.

Chloe went up to the bed and threw herself on it, lying down quietly and curling up like a little girl. She didn't know what to think. She didn't know what she was actually afraid of or worried about. When she had set off for Rio, she told herself she wouldn't allow anything to happen between herself and William. She couldn't afford to date again if her man was going to be a thousand miles away, but something had happened to her at the airport. She had felt her heart leap inexplicably when she walked in. That had never happened to her before. She hadn't ever felt that excited to see anyone in all her life.

That had lasted only until the blonde girl had come bursting onto the scene with her voice piercing the peace of the lobby and in Chloe's heart. If he had brought her to the airport, then he must have had a reason, and she thought it was telling her something.

"Who the fuck is still called Gertrude in this day and age?" she asked. The ladies burst into laughter, laughing raucously as they contemplated Chloe's question. She lay there, unmoving. Olivia walked to the window and stood, looking out at the crazy vista. The others sat around, resting their backs as they enjoyed the luxury of the suite that William had paid for.

"You ladies are missing quite a lot. This view is to kill for," Olivia quipped. They walked over, and she went to the bed and laid her hand on Chloe's shoulder. She understood how difficult it could be for a woman when the man she liked might just like someone else. "Why do you think he wants to take you out tomorrow?" Olivia whispered to her.

"He probably has a good schedule. Today is for Gertrude, while tomorrow is for me," she replied.

"Or, he wants to spend time with you because today is for whatever he's going to handle on the other side of the city."

"Maybe. I have been so unsure in the past. I don't want to waste my time worrying about a man. I'm too old for high-school drama," Chloe said.

"Yeah, it ain't working out very well for you, baby," Olivia said.

"No kidding. It's not working out at all. The jealousy I feel right here and now is just about enough to end me," Chloe said.

"You like him!" Olivia laughed.

"You better shut up," Chloe said as Olivia pulled away, laughing hysterically.

"Well, you got a bribe for me?" Olivia asked.

"You're in this fine-ass hotel because the man likes me. Isn't that bribe enough? The next man that likes me might invite me to Elon Musk's crib on Mass. Don't you want to come pay a visit and see how it is?" Chloe asked.

"What nonsense are you talking about? Bribe me properly before I spill all your secrets in public," Olivia demanded, that mischievous smile still sitting on the side of her lips.

"I'll give you a real ass whooping, Liv. You better keep your mouth shut," she said.

"Well, ladies, gather around. I have a story to tell you," Olivia announced.

"Okay, okay," Chloe said. "What do you want?" she asked.

"Just a little bit of open-mindedness, sweetness. Let me whisper it into your ear," Olivia said. She walked up and bent toward Chloe's ear, whispering lightly into it. "Go to William tomorrow with an open mind. Don't go assuming anything," Olivia said.

"That's going to be hard," Chloe replied.

"Keeping your secret is just as hard. That shit is trying to burst right out of my throat. I'm so tempted, but I have self-control," Olivia fired back.

"Okay, okay, I'll do it," Chloe agreed, shooting lasers at Olivia with her eyes.

"The two of you are full of shit," Ava said.

"I agree," Mia said.

"I'm sorry, sweethearts. When she fails to do the needful, I'll be happy to spill the beans on the matter, alright?" she said, returning to the window where the ladies still stood.

The waters of Copacabana sat placidly, shimmering in the evening light. There were people milling about on the waterfront. From their spot up there, they watched, enjoying the sight of the people, realizing that they would be those people in the coming days. The impeccable double suite was perfect for the five of them, and they ordered room service. It wasn't time to go out there, yet. It was time to enjoy the serene space with a perfect meal.

"What are we going for? Something local or continental?" Ava asked.

"I think continental. My body's clock is already messed up. Don't mess my taste buds up yet, please," Mia said.

"You might actually enjoy the local food more. Are you sure you don't want to have some fun?" Ava asked.

"Fun starts tomorrow, but tonight, I eat only what I'm familiar with," Mia said, stepping into the bathroom.

"I'm with Mia on this one," Chloe said.

CHAPTER 7

The heat of the day wasn't oppressive. The ladies spent most of their time walking the beachfront, enjoying the serenity of the beach as they took in the Copacabana area with the interesting games and fun things to do littered virtually everywhere they went. Ava and Mia joined a beach volleyball group for a quick game. Both of them had been on the volleyball team in college and still enjoyed the sport.

The others watched, enjoying the smile on Mia's face as she rose into the air to smash the ball right into the opponents' side. Her height offered her a slight advantage, but more important was the lift on her feet. She could jump higher than those who were taller than she was.

They walked to a small restaurant to enjoy some *moqueca*, a Brazilian fish stew that made Mia so happy she swore she would only eat that until they left town. They were just leaving the restaurant when William called to say he was on his way over. Chloe went back to the hotel to freshen up and get ready for the afternoon with him.

She wore a light navy-blue gown that stopped just above her knees. It was the perfect thing for this hot afternoon in Rio.

He drove her out of the immediate area, taking her back toward the embassy. He looked more dapper today than he did the previous day. He was dressed in plain black pants, a white shirt, and a brown jacket. She admired his clean-cut look, but it was that boyish grin that did a number on her. She couldn't resist that charming smile.

He took her to Lilia, a restaurant very close to the US consulate building in Rio. He ordered *brigadeiro* for her when she said she had eaten already. He said it was light and almost like a confectionary and she wouldn't even feel like she had eaten anything. For himself, he ordered barbecued meat that would sate him for the afternoon.

"How are you enjoying Copacabana?" he asked.

"It's a beautiful choice, and I'm not sure I've thanked you for getting that hotel for us," she said with a smile. Olivia had signaled her to have an open mind when she was leaving, reminding her of her promise.

"It's nothing. I had a room there before. I spent one night there some time ago when the barracks weren't working for me," he said. She thought about that. It might be his way of saying he went there with his women. She couldn't fathom what else that could mean. "I'm just glad you're here. I had hoped to spend more time with you in New York the last time I came around, but the unrest here meant I had to head back to work faster than I would've liked," he said.

"Duty, huh?" she quipped.

"Yeah, sometimes duty gets in the way of the most important duty of all," he said.

"What's that?" she asked.

"The duty we owe to those who are dear to our hearts," he explained.

She didn't want to push it, so she let it slide, unsure whether she would like to know who he cared about in this case. They spoke about New York, about the fashion industry, and about the unrest that his team had been brought in to quell. By the time the day wore on to evening, it was just like that one night in New York. They laughed and chatted with ease, enjoying the ambience of the quaint hotel and the meal.

"Do you want to get out of here?" he asked.

"Sure, where to?" she asked.

"I could show you around the embassy," he said.

"Wouldn't that be illegal?" she asked.

"Not if I get you a pass. Kids and others go on tour there all the time. You shouldn't be any different at all. Come on." He rose, dropped some money on the table, and grabbed her hand. They skipped, almost running, to his car. He drove down to the embassy. He parked his rental car in the parking lot and stepped out, opening her door and leading her around the embassy building. She smiled as they walked through and enjoyed the pride he took in showing her everything.

"Sarge, you're back?" a male voice came wafting through as they made it out of the main building. Chloe was wearing the visitor tag already. "Who is this charming lady? Won't you introduce me, Sarge?" he asked.

"Chloe, this is Henry. Henry, Chloe," William introduced.

"Oh, my pleasure, ma'am. So you're the Chloe he constantly talks about? He wasn't wrong at all," Henry quipped.

"What has he been saying about me?" she asked.

"Oh, many things, but the one that stuck with me is how you are so beautiful, he sometimes thinks you might be an alien or an angel," Henry said.

"Okay, that's it. Head on out, Henry. We'll head in the opposite direction," William said.

"But I want to listen to what he has to say," Chloe pleaded.

"I'm sorry, but his mouth is filled with lies. Don't believe anything he has to say," William said.

"Well, he wouldn't stop talking about your walk down the runway at a fashion event. He almost began to swear by your name then," Henry continued.

"Okay, that's it," William said, taking her hand and leading her away. She was struggling with him, laughing hysterically as they walked off.

"Don't be sore. He was only telling the truth. At least, I think he was," she said.

"Lies, all of it!" he quipped.

"Where do you guys sleep?" she asked.

"The team sleeps over there." He pointed at the lodging. "But I recently moved to the officer's mess. I can show you mine if you want to see it," he said.

"Yes, please," she said.

He took her over to his room. She smiled at the Spartan nature of the it: one wooden bed at one end, a television, and a small refrigerator made up most of the room. He pointed her to the only seat, a small couch resting against the wall, and grabbed a bottle of wine from the fridge.

He opened the wine and poured them each a glass. They sipped in silence for a while. Each time she raised her face from the glass, she found his eyes on her. She felt a little awkward at the desires that were flitting through her mind.

"Do you have any music around here?" she asked.

"I have this mixtape of my mother's that I carry everywhere with me. It has a list of all her favorite songs," he said, rising and popping a flash drive into a laptop connected to the television. A song came wafting from the stereo; it was Mariah Carey. Her "Without You" filled the room, and he stood watching the television screen. He walked over to her and gave her his hand. She took it, rising off the couch and holding him as they moved to the sound of the music.

She kissed him when Adele's "Make You Feel My Love" came on next. He pulled back a little, looking into her eyes. Then he went back in for the kiss. At first it was gentle, their hands roaming over each other's bodies softly. He pulled her close to him, pressing her to his center and kissing her even more passionately than before.

She looked up at him with lazy eyes and drew his head down toward her. Their lips met again, something that was fast becoming a habit that neither of them wanted to stop. Her lips were moist and soft, and he did not want to let go, but she pushed away. Then she led him to the bed. Her eyes, when they settled on him, told him something he always longed to hear. They said, "fuck me," and he knew this with certainty. He slowly pulled down her bra. His lips encircled the freed nipple, while his hand worked on unhooking her bra. It was out in five seconds, and he was sucking, listening to her moans. They filled the room.

He took her to the wall and made her lean against it, and then he went down on her, placing her right leg on top of his left shoulder. He felt her wetness through her panties, and she sucked in the air, gasping. He knew she liked it. Without wasting time, he pulled the little piece of clothing off of her and ran his tongue over her clit. Her fingers dug into his air as he did this, gripping tightly. He continued licking, sucking, kissing. Suddenly she pulled him up and away from her. He thought she was about to send him out of the room, but then she went down on him. Swiftly, before he knew what was going on, she had slipped out his hardness from his shorts and was now licking too, sending tingling pleasure along his spine.

He bent down and flipped her over so that she was upside down with her thighs on his shoulders and her mouth around his cock. It was easy. She didn't weigh much, which was part of what made her attractive. His tongue went in and out of her. When he rimmed her anally, she vibrated so much that he was afraid she would fall, but she held on to his hardness, slurping, licking, sucking. He was afraid he was already going to orgasm before getting to go into her. It felt so good. Her hands went around to his balls and squeezed lightly, and then she slipped a finger into his asshole. He staggered and fell on the bed, but she did not relent. It was like he was a meal that she had wanted to consume for so long, and all this time he had felt that he was the only one between them that felt an attraction. She pinned his two hands and sucked his cock to madness. When she was finally done, she rolled over and pulled him along with her.

"Are you sure you want to do this?" William asked, lying on top of her now, barely able to push back the curtains of want that was blocking out common sense.

"Fuck me," came the reply.

He was about to comply when Chloe tilted him over and sat astride. Then she produced a condom from thin air and deftly put it on him. She slid his erection into herself and began riding slowly. William felt her insides tighten against him as if giving his hardness a welcoming embrace. The feeling was electric. He seized the nipples in front of him and began sucking and kneading them. She was moaning now, a low sound that came from deep within her, escaping in a breath of pleasure.

"You're so big," she moaned.

William wanted very much to be humble, but he found himself grinning stupidly at what she said. Of course he was big. One thing he knew how to do very well was have sex.

With time, Chloe picked up the pace and was soon bouncing fast up and down William's cock. She pushed William away from her boobs and down to the bed before she grabbed his own nipples with her hands. She bent down after running her hands around them and took the right nipple in her mouth. It was an insane combination. With him still inside Chloe and her riding like that and still sucking his nipples, he was certain he was going to cum very soon. Sending his mind all over the place had no effect on his shaft; he could feel the eruption coming against his will. But the more he struggled against the sweetness that had him as a prisoner, the faster Chloe rode him till he groaned and let out his load. He curled up to grab Chloe's body and collapsed back on the bed after he was through the climax.

"Jesus," he said.

But even though she had won this round, Chloe wasn't done. She was on him again, biting his nipples ever so softly and teasing them with her tongue. Her hand ran along the length of his body to grab his now falling turgidity. She pulled the condom off and threw it to the side of the room, and then she began to run her hand along the length of the retracted penis. William sighed, satiated. He could feel her need for more of this, but he knew it was going to be a while before he was up and ready to fuck again.

When she turned in a sixty-nine position again, using her tongue to run along his length, he realized that he was having another hard-on. She had made him hard almost immediately. *Who was this?* he thought. This was not the quiet Chloe he knew from before. He rolled her over and raised her legs up. Then he bent them over. He began plowing.

"Ah," Chloe screamed when he hit particularly deep, clutching at his buttocks. He continued, going in rhythm with the country song playing through the stereo and sometimes going out of rhythm for effect.

Two minutes later, he let one leg down and continued plowing, and at the same time, sucked one of Chloe's nipples. She cried out in unbridled pleasure, totally clueless about what to do with her hands. They clutched at the bedsheets, dug into his hair, went up in the air, anything but stay in one place. Still, he did not stop. He pulled her hands together, finally letting down her legs, and held them above her head. As he fucked her, he sucked her nipples, sending signals scattering into various parts of her brain. She was screaming. She was moaning. She was squirming under him. Yet she could not get enough of him. The more she squirmed, the faster his rhythm went. He could feel her insides tightening against his hardness, announcing the coming of a climax. She was screaming more now. Then suddenly, the screaming stopped. She sighed, and her body loosened. The hole became freer. William stopped drilling.

He pulled her up and took her to the wall. There was a box, so he had her stand one of her legs on it. Then he slid in while standing. The next few minutes were filled with her pleasureful screams, his grunting, and naked skin hitting naked skin. She orgasmed again, this time, clinging to William's head so she would not fall. He took her to the bed and laid her there. It seemed like he had an agenda to make her mad with sex. He had Chloe bending in the doggystyle position as he slid in from the back. Each thrust hit the mark, and William had thrusts flying all over the place, clinging on to Chloe's butt. She was screaming and moaning, yet she wanted more. Again, William felt the tightening of her vaginal walls closing in on his hard shaft before they became free again. He continued, feeling his own release building up and close to explosion until he forced himself out of her, spilling all over the bed. They had forgotten to put on another condom. Either that or they just did not care about the condom at that point. William had never felt so close to anybody than in that moment. She turned around and collapsed on top of him. She was breathing hard, exhausted.

They sat around sipping wine and talking for a while. She walked about his small room naked, and he watched her, enjoying her dainty body and sensuous appeal. She made scrambled eggs, naked, and they sat on the floor to eat them, eventually putting their clothes back on.

There was something about this woman that called out to him to press hard on the brakes and take everything easy, but he wanted her more than anything in the world, and try as he might, he wasn't able to find those brakes to stop everything. Instead, he pulled her tighter into him, kissing her lips gently, his hands snaking about her, pulling her tighter into an embrace and running his hand over the small of her back. Her palm sailed through his shirt, caressing him gently, running up to his taut nipples, whispering pleasures through his pores.

Their passions came fast, like a tornado tearing through their whole beings. She tore at the buttons of his white shirt quickly, pulling them off and throwing them into the corner without a second thought. He grabbed the helm of her gown and pulled it up quickly, lifting the dress over her head. She stood there in her panties and bra, looking like a Victoria's Secret model. He gulped quickly, staring at her magnificent body. He couldn't fathom the magnificence. She watched his open mouth and the admiration in his eyes, and a smile came to her face, spreading warmly.

"My God! I haven't seen anyone as pretty as you," he said.

In response, she kissed him, sucking on his lower lip as her hands pulled at the buckle of his belt, pulling it off of him and pushing his pants down as he unclasped her bra, setting her boobs free from their encumbrance. Her hands ran down his taut abs, moving lower until they covered his cock. A short gasp escaped his lips as her hands made contact with his cock. She knelt down, sliding slowly while their eyes were locked on each other.

She pushed his underpants down quickly, releasing his hard cock from the confinement of his pants. It pointed straight at her face, veins sprouting on its sides, and she stared, awed by his magnificent cock. She wrapped her hand around his shaft, a gasp escaping him once more as she bent and kissed his tip softly, running her tongue around the bulbous tip of his cock. She took all of him in, her lips wrapping slowly around his cock, taking all of him deep into her mouth while her hand massaged his balls gently.

At first, she went in and out slowly, bobbing her head gently to the music of his pleasures. He closed his eyes, threw his head back, and caressed her body. She savored this ministration to his cock and enjoyed the moans escaping his lips. She sucked faster now, bobbing her head quickly on his shaft as his hand sailed through her hair, caressing, savoring her mouth around his cock.

When he couldn't take it anymore, he pulled her off the floor, slipping his hands under her arms and lifting her off the ground gently. She rose, kissing him quickly. Her lips tasted funny, but he didn't mind; he knew where her mouth had been. He laid her gently on his bed, kissing her softly, his palm caressing her boobs.

He bit softly into her neck as he kissed down there, traveling down to her boobs, taking her nipples into his mouth. He sucked quickly on one as his hand caressed the other, holding tight, speaking pleasures into her as she squirmed under him. He couldn't wait anymore.

He positioned his cock over her pussy, rubbing it gently over her wetness, caressing her clit quickly. She closed her eyes, anticipating that thrust, but he rubbed her up and down gently, making her squirm and whipping up her desire. When he thrust into her, a soft gasp of pleasure escaped her. He paused, savoring the pleasure of her pussy wrapped around his cock. For a moment, he didn't thrust into her. He paused, savoring the tightness.

He began to thrust gently, staring into her eyes as he thrust in. His palm slid up, cupping her face, holding her gaze, staring into those honey-brown eyes. He couldn't take his eyes away from hers, couldn't think of anything else in the world that could hold his gaze like this. She was everything, everything he could've imagined.

The gentle movement of his cock into her and the ebb when it came out was driving her mad. She couldn't contain herself. She was squirming under his weight, enjoying his deep ministrations, their bodies moving in tandem, like melody underlying the best music. Their moans rose together like incense, a sacrifice to whatever brought such pleasure. He thrust in deep, pulling out slowly until only his tip was left inside of her, and then he thrust in again, deeply, filling her up, causing her moans to become thrice more passionate.

He raised her off her back, laying her on her side while he lay close to her body, holding tight, pulling her close to him, thrusting back into her quickly with his hands wrapped around her. She moaned loudly as the pace of his thrusts became quicker. He caressed her boobs as he thrust into her, pinching her nipples ever so slightly as she gasped. He could feel her orgasm coming, and his wasn't very far away either. He drew her closer, thrusting hard and fast into her, causing her to squirm and call out his name.

When she announced her orgasm in a loud scream, he let himself go too. She held onto him, pressing him tight against her body as his orgasm rocked him. She kissed him, their lips tied together as their bodies stepped down from their crescendo. They stayed there in each other's arms, locked in that embrace that spoke louder than words.

"Want some more wine?" he asked after a while.

"Yes, please, I can drink more wine." She smiled. He got off the bed and grabbed the bottle they had ignored while engaged in reading the maps of their bodies. He poured it and sat, watching her face, enjoying the peace he saw on it. William felt himself drawn back on a journey through the past. He searched his memory, trying to discover a time when he had felt such overwhelming happiness, the type that filled him up with such bliss and made him feel like he was sitting right on top of the world. He couldn't remember a time like that.

"So, what do you guys really do on these assignments of yours? Sit around and enjoy the beaches and Rio women while waiting for the rebels to come off the mountain?" she asked. He chuckled.

"No, it's a little more complicated than that. For starters, I haven't met a Rio woman that appealed to me since I came down here. Second of all, sometimes when we get intel of the location of these bad eggs, we go out on an active hunt. It's how we've been able to capture a few of them," he explained with an indulgent smile hanging on his lips.

"How can you say Rio women have never caught your attention? I would do any of those women in a heartbeat if I were a guy," Chloe said, smiling mischievously.

"I guess you might if you didn't have something over your eyes. But if, like me, you've had your eyes elsewhere, on something much better than these women out here, then it wouldn't matter because you'd have seen better and desired better," he explained, staring at her, their eyes locked on each other. He stretched out his hand and cupped her cheek, caressing lightly and staring into her eyes as she lay, propped up on her elbow and staring straight ahead of her.

Chloe moved in for the kiss, a warm feeling spreading through her again as he spoke. She sucked on his lower lip, her hand rising to cup his face too, caressing softly, running over his soft skin as they locked lips. His hand strayed as he drew closer, cupping one boob, kneading gently, massaging her ample breasts and pinching the nipples lightly. He couldn't keep off. He drew closer, pushing her onto her back as he got on top of her, pinning her under him as he kissed hard, his hand straying to caress all of her.

The kiss strayed from her lips, moving down to her neck as if it had a mind of its own. It went beyond her neck, covering her boobs, sucking and biting softly on her nipples, tasting all of her. She closed her eyes, savoring the pleasure he whispered onto her body. He moved lower, kissing down her stomach, straying further downward, his inquisitive lips traveling past her belly button and down over her pussy. She expected to feel his tongue on her pussy, but he sailed past, kissing down her legs, pausing first to enjoy the pleasure of her thick, full thighs while his palm caressed her inner thighs, making her moan with pleasure. She moaned as he sailed past her thighs, going down her legs. He bit slightly into the fleshy shin as he sailed lower, kissing her feet, sucking gently on her toes. He looked at her to be sure she liked this, his eyes watching her through it all. Her closed eyes told him everything he wanted to know.

He took up the other foot and kissed it, traveling up its length, making pit stops here and there, savoring the taste of her until he returned to the inner thighs again. She squirmed under him as he teased her, kissing just around her pussy without diving into her.

When he did dive in, she wasn't expecting it, and an audible gasp escaped her. She wrapped her legs around his neck, pulling him in tight and holding him in as he sucked on her clit, his tongue sliding into her, making her gush with her juices. He grabbed her ass cheeks and pulled her to the edge of the slightly elevated bed. He sucked hard on her as she squirmed about underneath him.

He raised himself slightly, introducing a finger, then another. He caressed her pussy, making her squirm and move her body hungrily. When he drew his tongue over her clit one more time, she screamed his name, wrapping her legs tighter around his neck as her orgasm tore through her, making her sing with pleasure.

All the action had made his cock turgid with desire, and he rose, turning her around to push her onto her stomach. She gasped when he thrust into her from behind, burying his cock deep inside her. He thrust hungrily into her, his hands grabbing her boobs from his vantage point. She moaned with each thrust, her moans egging him on to satisfy her even more.

His gentle strokes gave well to a staccato beat when she pulled up into a moving position with him kneeling behind her, his hands grabbing a tight hold of her waist as he thrust into her. He didn't pause. He rose, lifting her up, his arms anchoring her legs as he held her against the wall, thrusting into her hard and fast. He kissed her, his tongue slipping through the parting of her lips to sail through her, unearthing the pleasures that were hidden deep within her.

She pushed him back, pointing to the bed and getting him back on it. He lay on his back with his cock pointing the way forward. She straddled him, impaling herself on his powerful cock. She could feel all of him and could control the tempo. She began immediately, rising slightly and falling back on his cock. She grounded into him, driving forward and backward, going around in an arc and repeating as he went wild, his eyes closed, his palms cupping her breasts as he could feel himself hurtling forward quickly toward orgasmic bliss.

"I'm going to cum," he warned.

"Me too!" she announced, throwing her head back and grinding harder into him. She rested her palms on his chest, staring at his face, taking in all of him as she felt the waves drawing closer. When the waves of her orgasm hit, she wrapped her hands around him, holding tight as her body convulsed with her orgasm.

They came together this time. Her yell of satisfaction triggered him, and he came, shooting his load into her. He held her in a tight embrace, their bodies locked deeply in sensual bliss. He didn't want to rise off the bed, and neither did she. So they stayed in each other's arms, savoring the afterglow of good sex. He couldn't recall having it this good before, and he wasn't in a hurry to let her go.

He pulled himself up to his elbows and stared into her face, enjoying the bliss as he looked at her face. Her eyes were closed, a small, satisfied smile sitting at the edge of her face in a blissful state. He stretched out a finger and caressed the side of her face.

CHAPTER 8

Chloe woke up in the middle of the night wondering where she was and what she was doing there. She could tell it wasn't the hotel; the sheets felt different, as did the bed. She looked around, trying to reacquaint herself with her surroundings.

It all came back to her like a jarring memory, and she sat up in the bed, her eyes roaming the room, trying to get adjusted to the dark. When she did, she could see a man's muscular body. He lay on his back, his left hand resting on his torso, his eyes closed placidly as he slept. She wondered what she had been thinking. She hadn't even texted or called Olivia and the others. She grabbed her phone and opened her messaging app. There were tons of suggestive emojis from her friends. She smiled, covering her mouth with her hand to stifle her laughter.

They must have created wild and fantastical images in their minds, and she couldn't fault them. She would definitely have to find a creative way to handle them when she returned to the hotel. If she didn't, she would probably have to find a different place to stay. Otherwise, they were going to tease her to death. She had fallen asleep without knowing, and William had probably thought it was a good idea to let her sleep. It was the jet lag. She should've taken the whole day to rest up.

This situation surprised her. She had created an elaborate plan, making sure she mapped it all out, detailing the possibilities of a sexual encounter with William and the ways she would escape in order to keep her sanity. But now she couldn't tell what came next. She had thrown everything out the window on the first date. She had even allowed him to shoot his load inside her.

"Good lord, what's come over me?" she asked herself, wondering how she had managed to completely lose control without a modicum of restraint in her body. She sat for a while staring at her phone, her eyes darting from the screen to the man lying in the bed. She could still feel the magnetism. And even now, with all these thoughts going through her mind, she wouldn't hesitate to jump on him again if he were awake.

She gave herself a mental slap and returned to the bed, lying slightly away from him so as to not make contact with his body because she was sure she wouldn't be able to control herself. She giggled excitedly. It had been a while since she felt this way about anyone. While she still felt she shouldn't have done it, she was glad she did. She closed her eyes.

When Chloe's eyes opened again, light was streaming in through the windows with the curtains parted at the sides. There was no one in the bed with her, and no one was in the room at all. She got off the bed and walked to the window. She could see a band of soldiers outside, lined up in a perfect square, with William at the head of the formation. He had on an army-green T-shirt and camo pants tucked into boots. His shoulders were even more prominent in the T-shirt.

When the soldiers began to jog out the gates and past the bend in the street, Chloe stepped away from the window. There was nothing for her to see anymore. The eye candy she had fixated on was gone, and she was left with nothing but an empty compound. She was startled when she turned around to find a lady standing by the open door. The door hadn't been open when Chloe had gotten out of bed, so this lady must have opened it. The familiarity startled her. What was she doing in William's room when he wasn't around? Did this mean she came around unannounced like this all the time? Otherwise, why would she do it when he wasn't there? Chloe comported herself quickly.

"You're the lady William came to the airport with," Chloe said without a smile. "May I help you?" she continued.

"I should be asking you that. Visitors aren't exactly allowed into this area of the embassy," she said, staring at her. She was relaxed, a smile sitting on the corner of her face as she faced Chloe, trying to unnerve her with her mannerisms. She walked into the room, impeccable in her appearance. Her pristine body made Chloe look herself over. She had William's sheets wrapped around her body, and her disheveled hair and morning face all made her feel inferior to this woman. The fact that she could waltz in here in this manner also made Chloe jittery. She wanted her gone.

"William isn't in. You should've come earlier or spoken to him outside when he was with the other soldiers," Chloe said.

"I came to see you, not William," she said.

"You should leave then. The exhibition is over," Chloe said and moved toward her. She walked past her and opened the door. Standing there, she waited with her hand on it.

"I'm Gertrude, by the way." she said, stretching her hand out to Chloe, who pulled the door further back, ignoring the outstretched hand. There was something about this woman that hadn't sat well with her from the first moment she had met her at the airport. Even now, watching her walk away before Chloe slammed the door shut, she had the same thought that something about her wasn't right. She walked back to sit on the bed, wondering who would name a woman Gertrude in the twenty-first century.

She looked around for her items of clothing. William had gathered everything and set them up on the only other furniture in the room. They were folded neatly, and this brought a smile to her face as she picked them up. She forgot about Gertrude for a moment and began to get dressed. Her phone rang as she was dressing, and she smiled, steeling herself up first before picking up the phone.

"Hi, Liv. Did I make you guys worry?" she asked.

"Oh, no, not at all. We spoke to William when you blatantly refused to take our calls." Olivia laughed. Chloe palmed her face, sure that it would be red with shame.

"How was it?" Ava chimed in.

"Oh my God," Chloe said.

"You better stop that. We want all the juicy details. Everything from how the heck did it begin to how was it." Olivia said.

"And then afterward, we would love for you to tell us what we should call you guys now." Avery snuck in that remark.

"Chloe and William, sitting in a tree, K-I-S-S-I-N-G," Mia sang.

"You lot need to grow up. I have to go now. You should act like adults by the time I get back," she said, ending the call. She palmed her face, laughing into it. She had known they would give her some hell, and this was only the mild version, probably because they feared William might be in the room. They would unleash true hell when she returned to the hotel room later in the day.

"Hey, beautiful," she heard a masculine voice call from the door. She looked up from the couch, her eyes catching William's at the door. He had a big smile on his face and two cups of coffee in his hands.

"Hey," she said, smiling.

"You were sleeping so peacefully when I left for the morning jog that I didn't want to wake you," he explained.

"That's okay. I watched you guys a little bit before you took off. Nice view from here," she replied.

"Well, these men are elite soldiers, and elite soldiers don't mess around with their workout routines. These guys are at the top of their game," he said.

"I was most interested in one of the guys, just one of them," she said, her smile broadening. His smile got bigger too, and she might argue that he was blushing, but he wouldn't agree with that sentiment. A hard-ass soldier like himself wouldn't be blushing at a woman's compliment.

"Why are you all dressed?" he asked.

"I have to head back to the hotel. My girls are waiting," she replied.

"We should have some breakfast before you leave," he said.

"I'll get something at the hotel. Don't worry about me. Just tell me how to get back, and I'll be out of your hair. I hear unauthorized personnel aren't supposed to be in here anyway," she said.

"Who told you that?" he asked.

"Oh, it was just something I overheard this morning," she explained, unwilling to tell him where she had gotten that information from. He was skeptical of the answer, but he didn't push it. He turned around and began to pull off his uniform.

"There's a fashion event coming up at the Hotel Rio Lancaster in a few days. I thought it might be something you'd like to go check out," he mentioned.

"Sarah Lavigne? I've heard about it. I've been thinking about dragging the girls to it," she replied.

"Oh, you already know about it? Will I ever be able to surprise you?" he asked with a smile.

"Not with a fashion event in a city I'm visiting. That's practically the first thing I look for before I travel to a city," she said, rising.

"I would still like to attend with you. You may not be walking the runway, but I liked how happy you were the last time I saw you at an event of that sort. Even with the little mishap, you still looked like you were having a lot of fun," he said.

"Oh God! I forgot you saw that!" she exclaimed.

"Well, it might have been less than perfect, but I still rate it an eight out of ten. That's how awesome you were at that event," he said. She felt herself blushing and turned away from him to hide her face. Her phone rang, and she picked it up. It was Olivia. Chloe listened for a little while before turning back to him.

"I should get going. The girls are getting very creative with their demands that I get back to Copacabana," she stated.

"Hold on. I'll call a cab to drive you back. I can't leave the embassy at the moment. My superior is unavailable hence I'm the highest-ranking officer here right now," he said.

The cab took her through the same streets they had taken the day before, but this time she allowed her eyes to roam. There were lots of tourists out, and she was able to recognize and differentiate them from the indigenes. This was becoming an easy thing for her to do because of all the vacations she had been on. Tourists were easy to spot because of their starry eyes. Everything was new and fresh to them.

When she walked into the lobby of Copacabana Palace, her eyes caught sight of the ladies immediately; they sat to the right as she made her way inside. And they weren't alone. Their companion had his back to Chloe, and she couldn't pin his identity down, but she had a strong feeling that she knew him. She turned and made her way to their table. Olivia's eyes caught her coming over, and she rose, calling out to her as she walked up.

The man rose. He was tall, dark, and every woman's wet dream. She paused when he turned around, her hand flying up to her open mouth as a wide smile spread across her face.

"Gary!" she called out, walking up quickly to fall into his arms. He gathered her, holding her tight against his strong frame. "Fucking Gary Lamont, what are the odds?" she asked.

"Not as small as you might think. For starters, I have a children's project I've been running over in Ecuador for a while now. And then there's Sarah Lavigne. If you've heard about that, then you know that the possibility of running into me here is quite substantial," he said in his deep baritone, wearing that famous indulgent smile on his face.

"Oh, well, I never really thought it through. How have you been, Gary? It's been, what? Four years?" she asked.

"Four years and five months," he said.

"That's quite precise," Olivia chipped in.

"Gary is nothing if not precise," Chloe said, staring into his eyes, watching his familiar face, feeling those familiar feelings as they came rushing back. She could remember how much of whirlwind he had been, all through her last two years of college. It had been Chloe and Gary at all the fashion events, winning every accolade possible at Kingsborough College and elsewhere.

She had met him at a fashion event, and they had hit it off immediately. Together they had ridden the whirlwind through those final two years at Kingsborough. Looking at him now, she could remember all the feelings and all the plans they had made together. Her eyes misted for a second, and she turned to face him.

"Where did you lot meet him?" Chloe asked excitedly.

"We were walking along the beach when we saw him. It was Liv who recognized him first," Ava answered.

"How's life treating you?" she asked him.

"Fairly good. Would you like to take a walk on the beach?" he asked, nodding toward the doors. Chloe left her purse with her ladies and walked down to the beach with Gary. As they walked, he spoke, carefully choosing his words as always.

"After Kingsborough, I knew the fashion scene wasn't where I aimed to stay. These days, I don't really walk much. I make appearances here and there on request, but my life is mostly spent working with kids. I teach, coach, and act as a life coach and guide.

"That has always been your dream. You've always wanted to walk away from the hustle and bustle of city life," she said. She could recall how this specific choice of his had been the deal breaker for them. She wouldn't agree to travel the world with him and volunteer for the rest of her life. That plan had never made much sense to her, and she had chosen to walk away instead of be the reason he didn't get to live his life the way he wanted to. He wouldn't bend, and neither would she, and so the best thing for them at the time was to part ways.

"Yes, but tell me how the fashion world looks now, not that I haven't followed your career trajectory. It pained me greatly that you chose to go into promotion and organization when we both know that you're a monster when it comes to walking and owning that runway. I was so elated when I found out just yesterday that you had made an appearance on the stage again. I didn't know I would see you today!" he said.

"You only found out yesterday?" she asked.

"Yes. Most times, I stay without a mobile phone for extended periods of time. I got myself one just yesterday to get on the internet and go through my emails. When I make my way back to Ecuador, if I do go back, I'll have to leave the phone here," he said. She could sense a sadness in his eyes as he spoke, and it piqued her interest. She wanted to know what was wrong, as this was not the same confidence she was used to with him. He was always boisterous and completely certain of his situation and the path he had chosen. This uncertainty was new, which was why she became immediately interested in it.

"What do you mean? Are you planning to head elsewhere for the same program?" she asked.

"No. I've been feeling slightly disillusioned and unsure about things. It's the reason I agreed to do this show. I feel like I missed out on something, like I didn't see my life through before attempting to help others see theirs. So my story feels incomplete. It's one reason I'm glad to have met you out here, because you are a part of that story." He paused now and turned to the water, staring off into the distant horizon. For a long time, he didn't say a word, and neither did she. They both watched the water, the people in it, and the vastness of it all. Everything felt a little surreal, like they were both in a time warp that had brought them to this point where they were hanging, unsure of what came next.

She turned and started walking along the sand; he fell into step beside her. She was angry, but she wasn't yet sure where that anger was coming from. All she knew was that she was so angry that she wanted to lash out at something.

"Are you walking at Sarah Lavigne?" he asked.

"No," she replied.

Another awkward silence stretched out endlessly in front of them. They still walked, but without words. They had actually done this many times: walking, saying very little, and simply enjoying each other's presence.

"Do you miss us?" he asked out of nowhere.

"There is no us, Gary," she said. There was no smile on her face. "How's your mother?" she asked after a while.

"She's alright. I haven't seen her since last year. That was the last time I was in Nebraska. She hasn't aged much. She's still strong enough to yell the skies down if she wants to," he said. Chloe chuckled at that, recalling the few times she had gone home with him. His mother had been pleasant to Chloe, but she wasn't a very pleasant person to other people.

"She can really yell; it's almost like a superpower," she said.

"But she never yelled at you. In her eyes, you could never do any wrong." He laughed.

"You were her most prized possession, and she wasn't going to risk scaring away your female friend. It wasn't me she liked; it was you." Chloe replied. He didn't say anything for a while.

"She asked about you the last time I spoke with her," he finally said.

"Why? She hasn't asked about me in the past four years, has she?" Chloe asked.

"I guess not, but she mentioned you the last time we were talking on the phone. I send her emails and letters, but when I arrived in Rio, she was my first call," he said.

"Good for you," Chloe said.

"I would love to see you walk the stage here in Rio; it would be a bit like the old days," he said.

"That's not going to happen. My comeback was a bit of a disaster, and I won't be making an appearance like that again," she said.

"You were excellent. I've watched that video over and over. Whatever made you trip wasn't about your gait or control; it was something in the audience. I could see you looking out there like you were searching for something or someone," he said.

"How could you know that?" she asked in surprise.

"I've walked the same stages with you for a very long time. I know you, Chloe," he answered.

She turned abruptly and walked back toward the hotel, leaving him standing there, staring after her.

"Chloe, wait!" he called, but she didn't stop, and he didn't chase after her. He knew her well enough, and running after her would only make matters worse. He stood there, watching as she walked away, almost the same way she had watched him walk away those long four years ago. He could guess now how she had felt then, but now he wasn't sure how he planned to achieve his aim in Rio. He had been out of touch for far too long, and getting all the magic back again might be difficult. But he had come because he wanted to try and see how everything went.

Things might be uncertain, but Sarah Lavigne's show was the

place to begin. He smiled and picked up some pebbles, throwing them with some expertise into the water, watching the ripples and smiling to himself.

CHAPTER 9

"**S**ergeant Hanley, I have been patient with you over the past few weeks, but you have refused to do what you know you ought to do," Gertrude Winter said, blocking William's path as he made his way to his room after the morning's jog.

"I don't need therapy, ma'am." He walked forward, almost brushing past her in the process. She stepped aside, but in the distance he could see Major McCaw. The major gave him a look before walking over to where he stood. He was unsure of what his next move should be. William hated all types of therapy. He thought they were a waste of time and that a man should be able to take whatever punch nature dealt him without complaining or bitching to a shrink who probably knew nothing about the situation.

"Sergeant Hanley, Gertrude informs me that you have not yet availed yourself of the opportunity Uncle Sam is offering to let you get some heavy things off your chest. Can you tell me why?" he asked.

"Therapy is for sissies, sir!" he said, saluting.

"I know that, son, but Uncle Sam pays Gertrude here to provide you with all the therapy you need, and you might as well take it so the money doesn't go to waste. Do you understand?" he asked.

"Yes, sir!" William replied.

McCaw turned on his heels with a nod to Gertrude Winter and made his way back to his office. William turned around and followed the therapist to her office. He walked like a man with a rope tied unwillingly around his neck, like a sacrificial animal. Her office was small, with very little personal touches. He was surprised. For a woman, that was extremely unusual.

"You aren't much for decoration," he commented.

"Sharp eyes. That's an excellent quality in a job like yours. What else do you notice?" she asked.

"You've added very few personal touches here, which tells me you aren't much of a people person. Actually, I've always thought you were shit with people, and this just confirms my suspicions," he said.

"And here I was, thinking I would be the one to give *you* therapy," she quipped.

"I guess Uncle Sam should probably divert your paycheck to my bank account," he said. She laughed, a bit more than was appropriate for the situation, which caused William's eyebrows to furrow.

"You have jokes," she said. "Now sit, and let's begin," she said, taking her seat and waving him into one. He sat, folded his hands across his lap, and stared at her. She watched him, her eyes boring holes into him.

"What do you consider the worst handicap for a soldier in an assignment of this type?" she asked.

"What type?" he asked.

"You, here, now. What do you think of it?" she asked.

"I have a job to do, and I will do it and go home, or wherever else there is a job for me to do. That's all there is to it," he said.

"So you don't mind the half-naked women walking around the numerous beaches here? You'd remain focused in the face of all of that?" she asked, staring sternly.

"The job comes first," he replied.

"Then you wouldn't mind telling me why you brought a woman to the base and kept her here overnight?" she asked.

"How did you find out about that?" he asked.

"I know everything that goes on around here, and I should let you know that nothing escapes me," she said.

"Good to know," he replied.

"Why bring a woman here if you don't exactly mind the presence of voluptuous and available women surrounding you?" she asked.

"She's a friend. She came down to Rio from New York on vacation. By the way, where does it say that bringing a woman to my quarters is a crime?" he asked.

"It breaks all the rules of etiquette. And what does it say to your men? Go to town on these Brazilian booties?" she asked.

"Since you put it that way, there is no man among my group who would be willing to take you up on that offer. They know what they are here for. And sex is a natural need for men; it's not a crime. But I speak for myself when I say my work matters more to me than some pretty butt in the sand." He rose, smiling indulgently at her. "If there is nothing else, I should probably get to the bathroom and wash off this sweat," he said.

"Are you sure it's just the bath you want to go in there for?" she asked.

"What?" he asked.

"Never mind," she said, rising. "I will see you again tomorrow at the same time, so we can get a full hour in."

"This hasn't been enough madness for you already? What is it you want from me?" he asked angrily. For a moment, he watched as her eyes roamed all of his body, staring, taking everything in, savoring the masculinity he was coated with. Her eyes crinkled, and her lips curled up to the side. "Do you not have anything to say?" he asked.

"Tomorrow, same time. If you happen to miss it, you might be on your way out of Rio by evening," she stated. He stood there, staring at her, anger coloring all the emotions that streamed out of him. He hadn't been this angry in a very long time, and he knew he had to leave the room immediately, or he risked doing something he might later regret.

He walked out of her office, immediately making his way toward his room. He could feel himself burning up. He hadn't ever been in army therapy before, but he had never thought this was how it was done. As he turned the corner, he found a pretty figure standing at his door, her hand folded across her bosom.

"Chloe?" he called tentatively. She turned around and smiled broadly, her face holding happiness that immediately permeated his being, and he forgot the anger that had been in his chest just moments ago. "What are you doing here?" he asked.

"I just wanted to see you. I know you're busy and all, but the girls were talking about going sightseeing. I didn't feel like it, so I chose to come here instead," she explained.

"I love that you're here," he said, hugging her tight and sniffing her hair as she leaned in. He bent slightly and kissed her, their lips grazing ever so slightly before he straightened up and led her into his room. When he opened the door and drew her in, she had a quizzical look on her face.

"Shouldn't you have returned from your jog about an hour or so ago?" she asked.

"Compulsory therapy. Gertrude is having a field day demanding that I attend that shit or be forced to leave Rio by tomorrow evening. Can you imagine that madness?" he asked.

"Oh, they're making you receive therapy? I thought therapy was supposed to be a good thing?" she quipped.

"Not for me. I don't sit around talking about the things I'm feeling," he said. "Why are we talking about Gertrude? Come over here," he said, pulling her to him and bending to kiss her lips lightly. She leaned into him, enjoying the feeling of his lips on hers. A smile played across her face as he caressed her body, his strong hands roaming the small of her black as his lips kissed her passionately.

He lifted her off the ground, feeling his desire rage within him, staring into her honey-brown eyes. He was always lost in them, her eyes taking him in and ensconcing him in their mysteries.

"You're beautiful," he said.

"You're even more beautiful," she quipped.

He ran his finger over her cheek and down over the length of her neck, tickling her skin, making her feel something she had never felt before. She moaned his name, her hand rising to cup his face as she kissed him, his moans escaping slightly through his breath. Her hand ran over his body, sliding to the small of his back and pressing him into her.

"You complete me," he said, turning on the music and pulling her toward him.

He drew her to him and kissed her lips passionately. She laid her palm on his chest and ran it along his rock-hard abs.

He grabbed her ass and pulled her into him, making sure she felt the touch of his cock. He walked to the bed and sat, leaving her in the middle of the room. She was confused at first, but then he motioned toward his groin. She got down on her knees and quickly opened his zipper. Placing both hands on his pubic area, she moved them gently, her face holding that look of awe for his magnificent body. She grabbed a hold of his rock-hard cock, and her eyes widened at how huge he was.

She kissed it, running her tongue around the cap and then slowly taking his shaft into her mouth. She placed her hand around the base of his cock so she wouldn't have to take it all in. He could feel the tingling sensation of pleasure as her mouth enveloped him, and a soft moan escaped his lips. She enjoyed the feeling of his cock in her mouth, and she found herself pressing her boobs against it. She wanted to worship this cock, make it feel like the only cock in the universe.

She went to work, bobbing her head up and down his shaft. He held on to her blonde hair and fucked her throat, thrusting into her mouth until she gagged and sputtered. He pushed her back and undressed her slowly, his eyes taking all of her in. She had a beautiful body that she often hid in baggy clothing.

She was beginning to enjoy herself. She wiggled her hips, letting her dress slide off her body in slow motion. When it fell around her legs, she was left in her black panties and bra. She unclasped the bra gently, taking it with one hand and throwing it aside. Then she began to push her panties down sensuously, wiggling her hips as they slid down to her feet. She stood there with her hand covering her mound, her perky boobs pushing out further.

William swiveled her around and thrust into her quickly, pushing her against the wall. Bending, he put his lips against her pussy and tasted the sweet juice of her arousal. He sucked her clit softly, running a finger through her as he kissed her opening, enjoying the taste of her nectar this early in the morning. She moaned, calling out his name as he ate her pussy. Her legs felt like they couldn't hold her much longer as the pleasure tore through her. He then rose in one swift movement and buried his cock into her pussy. She gasped when his huge dick stretched her out, and then she smiled with satisfaction as he began to thrust into her slowly.

She moved with him, bucking her hips to meet his thrusts. He encircled his strong right arm about her body, grabbing a hold of her left boob and kneading it as he thrust into her. Her moans wafted like music into William's ears. He enjoyed the sounds of her pleasure.

He swiveled her around and pushed her down to her knees. Then, mounting her like a steed, he thrust deep into her, filling her up. Her moans became louder as he went faster, dropping his slow thrusts for much faster ones. She yelled for William as spurts of her juices gushed out of her.

He pushed her to the side and lifted her right leg up, slamming into her as hard as he could from behind. She was thrashing about the bed as he slid in and out of her pussy, fucking her so hard she couldn't hold herself any longer. She could feel the waves of her orgasm overtaking her body. Her hips were on fire, and words escaped her lips as she yelled her arrival. But he wasn't done with her yet. He pulled her up into a kneeling position and slid back into her. Grabbing her waist for support, he slammed deep into her, making her scream with the pleasure of his hard thrusts.

His moans came frequently now, deep and guttural like an animal's. She pushed back on him, meeting every one of his thrusts squarely. The music their bodies made was like the lovemaking scene of age-old lovers who couldn't get enough of each other.

He turned her around, raising her left leg onto his arm, he slid into her pussy while still standing and thrust deep into her. She squirted even more, yelling as another orgasm overtook her. He kept thrusting into her.

The sounds of their pleasureful moans wafted up. William's

voice climbed a notch higher than before as he felt himself close to the edge. He thrust deeper, pressing his palm against her pussy to rub her clit and stimulate her even more. She immediately screamed her orgasm, and he pulled out of her, holding his cock in his hand. She fell on her knees quickly, and he shot his load into her mouth. She sucked him off, slurping over his cock as she enjoyed his juice.

But he still wasn't done. He was up in moments, hungry to taste her juices, to feel her squirm under him.

He pushed her back against the wall, bending to take her lips with his, kissing her passionately, his hand snaking through her lush hair. He could feel her desire in the urgency with which she kissed him back; it was in the fire that blazed in her pupils and snaked out through her lips. He could feel it in the tightness of her arm around his body. He pushed her further into the wall, like foam, his hand roaming her whole body, grabbing one boob and squeezing hard.

When he bent and kissed her neck, she moaned deeply, sucking in her breath. He drew her away from the wall, moving her back on the bed. He bent over her steamy mound in one swift movement. His hand rested hungrily on her boob while his mouth sought the sweetness of her pussy. He could feel his cock throbbing beneath him again.

He savored her scent, running his tongue along her inner thighs, kissing down her legs to her knees and back up again. He could feel her need; she placed her hand on his head and tried to pull his attention to her center. But teasing her felt like a more rewarding option, so he trailed the other leg, kissing down to her toes.

"Please, Will," she pleaded.

He bit lightly on her thigh as he kissed her from her toes back to her steamy center. It was killing him, the scent of her arousal swirling around his nose. He stuck his mouth on her pussy. Her gasp was a satisfying reminder that she had waited eagerly for this. He kissed along the edge of her pussy lips, running his tongue quickly over her exposed clit. She moaned, her fingers raking through his hair as the pleasure hit her center.

He grabbed both of her butt cheeks and pulled her closer, gaining a tighter hold of her. He fucked her with his tongue, snaking it in and out of her hole slowly, in that teasing motion that she liked. She gasped louder than she had done before, a sure sign that he had gotten to her.

"I want you, William," she said.

He sucked harder on her clit, working his finger right on the top of her mound. He could feel her sharp intake of breath as the pleasure mounted.

He rose to take her mouth, sure that his face was wearing her juice as makeup. He kissed her lips, giving her a taste of her own pussy. She kissed him with urgency, his throbbing cock dangling just inches from her pussy. She grabbed it and placed it at her entrance.

"Please . . ." she begged.

He pushed in, her words ending in a gasp. His thrusts were slow and deliberate, pulling all of his dick out until only the tip was left in her before sliding back in again. Each thrust drew a gasp and a moan from her, and his pace began to pick up quickly. The slow rhythm progressed to a fast beat as he tore into her pussy, moving in and out of her, the pleasure climbing through his shaft as her tight pussy caressed it.

He bent and took her nipple in his mouth as he thrust deep into her. She was squirming under his tight hold, her moans rising like sweet music to his ears. Her fingernails tore into William's back as his thrusts grew into a frenzy.

He swiveled her in a fluid motion, bringing her on top without sliding out. She began a smooth movement, bouncing her pert ass on him, managing the pace now while her palms rested on his chest. She began to grind into him. William could feel her ass and the increased tightness as she threw her head back and rode him. He began to push back, meeting each of her thrusts. He grabbed a hold of her boobs and thrust deep into her.

She got up and knelt on the bed, lifting her ass sensuously.

William knelt behind her and slid his cock in. Grabbing a hold of her waist, he began thrusting into her, going faster and faster as she yelled for more. He hit her deep and hard, feeling his orgasm close by. He placed his hand on the top of her pussy and worked her clit, slapping it hard as the thrusts increased. He grabbed one boob and pinched the nipple hard. The overwhelming pleasure overtook her. He could feel the trembling of her legs as her orgasm washed over her. He pulled his cock out very quickly and shot his load there on the sheets.

"I think we've become some kind of animals," Chloe said.

"You do that to me," he panted.

They lay there, sneaking back into each other's arms and holding tight. William tried to think back to the first time he had seen this woman, to recall the thought he had about her. But all he could think about was how much he enjoyed being with her.

"Is it time I called you my girlfriend?" he asked.

"Boyfriend wouldn't sound so bad either," she said and giggled.

CHAPTER 10

Chloe got very little sleep that night, as she was troubled. Memories flooded her mind, making her unable to rest peacefully. Gary popping up again into her life wasn't such a big deal, yet it was troubling her so much, and she wasn't sure how she would hand it. It had completely disrupted her sleep. She thought of walking down to the hotel bar and helping herself to some alcohol, but Gary was staying in the same hotel, and she didn't want to run into him again.

She went to the minibar in their suite and grabbed herself a bottle of whisky and a shot. She went to the small balcony overlooking the beach and sat, watching the water. There were still quite a few people down there at this hour of the night. She shook her head as she thought back to that time after college had ended. They had made all kinds of plans and even went house hunting for over five weeks. But when they finally found a place, Gary came up with this idea of serving the world first before settling down to his life.

"You're drinking alone?" Olivia asked, making her way over to the where Chloe sat.

"Couldn't sleep either?" Chloe asked.

"I didn't get to speak to Carlo tonight. He's been at the office, and I find it difficult to fall asleep if I don't get to speak with him before I go to bed," she said.

"Aww, love birds. But how do you explain our insomnia, considering we don't have any lovers to fret over?" Avery asked, joining the other two.

"My guess would be that you're worried about your situation and probably scheming about how to snag some man somewhere." Olivia laughed. Then she saw Chloe throw back another shot of whisky, and she turned quickly, worried about her friend.

"Chloe, is everything alright?" she asked.

"Gary's a bastard. He's always been. I just never paid attention," she said.

"What did he do?" Avery asked.

"He wants to live his life again after wasting four years meandering through the woods, destroying the good thing we had. He's saying he thinks he might have made a mistake. Where does that leave me? What does that offer me?" she asked, on the verge of tears.

The others were quiet, watching her as she fought valiantly to keep the tears at bay. She threw back another shot, and Avery grabbed the bottle.

"That's enough," she said.

"You don't understand, Avery. Do you remember Gary and me? How perfect we were for each other? How perfect we were in every fucking way? Goddamn it! We were the stuff of stories, but he had to head off into the bushes with his big dreams and other bullshit."

"He doesn't matter anymore, Chloe. You have William now. He's solid. He's everything you'd want except the part where his work also keeps him away for longer than you'd like. But then, you spent the night with him, and isn't that magnetic enough for you?" she asked. Chloe smiled slightly.

"There was definitely some magic in there, I tell you," Chloe replied.

"Come, you owe us a story. We haven't gotten it out of you yet," Avery said.

"There isn't much to tell. We ate at a restaurant, and then he took me back to the embassy and showed me around. Then we went to his room and lost track of time," Chloe said, bursting into mischievous laughter.

"You all bumped uglies." Olivia clapped.

"We definitely did!" Chloe laughed.

Alright, come on now. You need to get to bed and catch some zees," Avery said, leading Chloe over to the bed and tucking her in.

"Kiss me goodnight, Avery. You look so pretty, I could literally eat you up."

"Liv, how much is left inside that bottle?" Avery asked.

"Just a quarter of the original amount," she replied.

"Damn! She drank everything?" Avery asked.

"Almost," Olivia replied.

"She's in bed now, and your phone is ringing. I'm guessing your man is out of his meeting," Avery said to Olivia, who rushed in quickly, grabbing her phone and placing it against her ear. Her broad smile spoke volumes and brought a smile to Avery's face too.

***

It was a soft knock on the door that woke them all up in the morning. They woke up groggy, ready to tear into the heathen knocking at their door so early. Olivia, who only slept a little in the wee hours of the morning, was the angriest. Chloe felt like a hammer was slamming into her head when she heard the noise. They would have all loved to ignore the knocker, but when he knocked again, they knew they had to answer or risk being kept awake if it persisted. Ava, who was closest to the door, rose and grabbed the doorknob.

"Oh, hey, it's you," she said, pleasantly.

"Yes! You look so pretty when you wake up," a deep, masculine voice said from the door. The sound piqued Chloe's interest, and she got off the bed and ran to the bathroom to keep herself out of sight.

"Is Chloe here? I have some news for her," he said.

"Yeah, sure, let me get her. By the way, you don't look so bad yourself for a man who just got out of bed," she said, smiling as she turned away. "Where's Chloe? Gary's looking for her," Ava said. Chloe poked her head out of the bathroom, waving both hands in a gesture that clearly stated she didn't want to see anyone.

"Why?" Ava mouthed. Chloe kept waving her hands, and Ava returned to the door.

"Gary, it seems Chloe stepped out earlier, just before you came in," she said.

"Oh, that's alright. I wanted to give her this news myself, you know? Get to enjoy the elation on her face when she hears that Sarah Lavigne would love to have her at the show next week. I know how much that news would mean to her," he said, deliberately raising his voice to draw attention.

"What did you just say?" Chloe asked, stepping out of the bathroom and moving quickly to the door where Gary stood with a mischievous smile on his face.

"I thought you weren't in?" he asked, still smiling.

"Who said I wasn't in?" she asked.

"Ava, just now. Anyway, it doesn't matter. Sarah Lavigne contacted me about walking the runway, and I told her I wouldn't do it unless you're going to be walking with me," he explained.

"And?" she asked anxiously.

"And she said yes, of course. What else could she have said?" he asked.

"You're never one to lack confidence. I'm glad you remembered me," she said, hugging him.

"How about a walk along the beach? We could practice the moves while we walk?" he said.

"Sure, I'll just clean myself up and brush my teeth," she said and shut the door in his face. Running back into the suite, her girls were all eyes and all ears, waiting to hear her thoughts.

"This could be the beginning of my return to the runway. The last one I did was a little off, but this would be different with all of you by my side and with Gary! We could conquer the fashion world again, just as we had always planned to do," she said.

"This is a big deal, Chloe! Congratulations!" Olivia quipped.

"Thanks, Liv!" she said, rushing into the bathroom. She was brushing her teeth when Ava walked in.

"Why were you hiding from him earlier?" she asked.

"I was confused, and I still am. I keep asking myself why he's here right now, trying to be in my life. He said a few things before that makes me think this meeting is no coincidence. I don't have a handle on what's going on, so I was planning to be careful with him, keep my distance and all that. Things with William are getting interesting. I don't usually sleep with the men I go out with after just two dates, but I have slept with William twice! And we haven't even had a proper date yet!" she said.

"You went on two dates already: one in New York, and the other here," Ava said.

"Those aren't proper dates, though. You know how these things work. But he makes me feel a certain way. Everything seems so effortless with him. Yet I don't know," she said.

"We'll talk more when you return. Just go, and finalize this Sarah Lavigne thing," Ava said as Chloe stepped out of the bathroom. Gary leaned off the wall and stretched out his hand to her as she made her way out of the room.

"You look so pretty," he said.

"I've always looked pretty, Gary. I didn't even put any makeup on my face. What you have here is a classic facial-wipe situation." He held her hand as they descended to the ground floor. They walked the lobby before going out to a coffee spot on the beach. The barista there was a young girl with large eyes that twinkled when she laughed. Gary had a lot to laugh about with her, and it helped Chloe relax with him. He led her off to a rocky part of the water where they would sit and watch people on the beach. He sat first, inviting her to do the same.

"You never really got to catch me up on your life the other night," he said.

"I thought you wanted to give me details on the Sarah Lavigne show?" she asked.

"Sure, we'll get to all of that. But right now, I want to get to know you again, learn whatever I didn't know before," he said.

"Like what?" she asked.

"Did you ever get that master's degree you always talked about? Did you get to travel the world like you've always wanted? You were always full of dreams and aspirations. You weren't one to just lay low. You've always been a go-getter. I just want to know if that person is still in there," he said.

"I have visited some of the cities on my bucket list, but I haven't gotten that master's degree. Life happened. Sometimes, I feel a part of me died when you left. But I've kept the push alive. The goal is to move forward no matter what comes my way," she replied.

"Any boyfriend?" he asked.

"Maybe, maybe not. Now, let's talk about Sarah," she replied.

"Oh, you have absolutely nothing to worry about. You have this down pat and will be able to walk it with relative ease. Are you worried about repeating the small mishap in New York?" he asked.

"Not really. Like you said, I had my mind on something other than my walk, and I ended up in that situation. But besides that, I don't fear the runway. I have never feared the runway, so I'm very sure everything will work out well," she said.

"Then we can spend our time talking about other things besides the event. I mean, haven't we been apart long enough? Don't you think we should talk about more important things like who we are now? Where do we think we will be in the next five or six years? Because I see us taking over all the major stages in Europe!" Gary said.

"I like the energy you're bringing to this newfound belief of yours; it's really captivating. Let's see how Sarah Lavigne's event goes, and then we can decide how we wish to proceed," Chloe chimed in.

"Visualize, Chloe. It's how we've always done it: we see it first, and then we go ahead and make it happen!" he said. She nodded, recalling their breathing exercises on the eve of a big event. She remembered how they often took walks together, discussing an event, trying things out, critiquing each other's steps and making sure they were ready. It was part of the reason why they were so good together, always working and acting as each other's support systems. While she thought about this, she recalled how he had left, throwing away all they had worked for, all they had planned.

Even now, as the anger welled up inside of her, she realized that this was not the time to get angry. Instead, it was the time for her to work toward rebuilding all she had lost. And the first step toward that rebuild was to work with Gary to re-create that power they had at the beginning. And that began here, with this coming event.

"I would really love to do the breathing exercises again, Gary. Do you think we can bring it all back?" she asked.

"Definitely. We can bring every single bit of it all back. Let's start with the breathing exercises," he said.

***

William Hanley walked into Gertrude's office with a scowl on his face. He was angry. This therapy was not for him, and he had told that to anyone who would listen. Left to him, all therapists would cease to exist, but he didn't have that power. So he played the hand he was dealt. The moment he walked into Gertrude's office, his countenance changed. He could see that the lady was in some form of discomfort.

She held one of her arms, pushing it over her other hand and pressing it hard. He wondered what had happened to her, and as was his nature, he rushed forward, eager to find out what the problem was.

"What happened?" he asked.

"I hurt my shoulder," she said.

"How?" he asked.

"I don't know. I was trying to pick out a book from up there, and the next thing I know is I'm here, struggling with my arm," she said.

"Come, I have something in my room that will help," he said, leaning in and gathering her around his shoulder as he led her out of the office. They made it to his room, and he led her to a chair, helping her to sit gently.

"Ouch, ouch," she complained.

"What is the problem?" he asked.

"The chair is too tight for me; it's making me feel even more pain," she said.

"That's the only furniture in here. Come, lay on the bed," he said, leading her to the bed and laying her down gently. She was still whimpering as he laid her down." He walked to a cabinet and picked out a small plastic bottle filled with oil. He knew her shoulder couldn't really be dislocated, but she must have banged it hard and could use a massage. He knelt beside her and took a hold of her shoulder, rubbing it gently, getting ready to massage it with the ointment when his phone rang. He got off the bed and grabbed the phone. It was Major McCaw.

"I need you to take two guys and head to town. There's a development you'll need to handle there. Get moving!" the major ordered.

"Yes, sir!" William replied and ended the call. He began to rush out and make his way to the compound.

"Are you going to leave me here?" Gertrude asked.

"I'll be back promptly. Just make yourself at home," he said. "Alternatively, I can send the resident physician to take a look at your shoulder," he suggested, rushing back into the room.

"No, I don't want anyone to see me in this condition," she replied.

He raced out of the building, grabbed a few men, and drove into town. Gertrude, meanwhile, made herself very comfortable. First, she took off her shirt, exposing a lacy black bra that looked appetizing. She had ample boobs that defied gravity and pointed straight toward the sky. The bra held them up perfectly. Then she relaxed. After a moment, she felt a need to make an adjustment: her bra was a little too heavy, and she didn't want to have it on anymore. It was an easy decision since she was sure she could already hear William's shoes clapping against the floor outside the room. She unhooked her bra and lay back on the bed, covering herself up with his sheets.

When the door opened slightly, she jerked up and made a go for her bra, but she was a little too late. He would have to go out again and allow her to put her bra and shirt back on. She dreaded a scenario where the person coming in was one of the other soldiers. They would gossip about this forever.

"Oh, it's you," she commented when she saw Chloe standing there with an incredulous look on her face. For a moment, Chloe couldn't believe her eyes. She just stood there watching the woman in William's bed. Then, tired of being rooted to this spot, she walked over to where Gertrude lay in the bed and grabbed the sheets, flinging them off of her sharply.

"You didn't have to do that!" Gertrude yelled.

Chloe turned around immediately and stormed out of the building. She whipped out her phone and wrote William a scathing text. She had come to him hoping to share her good news with him, but he wasn't there. Instead, he had left a half-naked woman in his bed for her to find.

The pain caused her eyes to water, blinding them as she made her way to the rental car she had had to get because of the commute from Copacabana. She drove back to the hotel in tears.

As she trotted inside, Gary was sitting at the bar alone. He beckoned to her, noticing her distress and quickly expressing his concern. He pulled her into an embrace, and she found herself falling apart. She couldn't even say two words before she broke down.

"Shh, tell me what the problem is, and we'll get through it together," he consoled, leading her off to his room. He could already think of the reason for her tears. It had to be a man. Only a man could do this to a woman.

All through the night she cried, wondering how she had become so lost. She had slept with William twice already, and then he went and did this. She couldn't explain it, but he was now acting like all the other men she had come to know. They were always the same: always shitty, always overly selfish. Gary was careful. He didn't attempt to touch her. Instead, he provided succor, whispering consolation into her ears, making her feel like everything would be alright.

She went back to her room later that night, and he promised to see her in the morning. His dream was coming to fruition gradually. It might take a while, but it was gradually coming to be.

CHAPTER 11

As the sun chased its own tail across the expanse of the sky in the early hours of the morning, Gary began to ready himself. He knew how to get Chloe to forget whatever she may have felt for the man who had broken her heart in this manner. He thanked Providence in his heart, happy to have another opportunity.

He was up in the ladies' room very early, knocking excitedly. It was Olivia who opened the door. Standing there, she stared at him, watching him for a while without words. She didn't like him, and he had seen that a long time ago.

"I came for Chloe. We made some plans last night to help her get back on her feet again," he said.

"Why are you doing this benevolent thing?" she asked.

"She's my friend, and no matter what happens, she's always going to be my friend," he confessed. Olivia clucked her tongue and shut the door in his face. She walked back to where Chloe was dressing and whispered into her ear.

"You have to be careful with Gary. He looks a lot like a right crook," Olivia said to Chloe.

"Way ahead of you," she replied.

He took her out to his all-terrain vehicle and helped her get in. He knew what he wanted to show her. He wanted her to explore Rio beyond what she had seen already. So he drove first to Tijuca where they saw one of the notable Brazilian festivals in its full bloom.

From the colorful clothing to the dances and the drumming, everything looked so real. And Chloe found herself admiring the culture and appreciating the people she had been living amongst. It was beautiful.

From there, he drove them to the Selaron Steps that marveled of nature where the artist had put both his heart and craft together to create one of the most beautiful mosaics ever seen. Chloe was speechless when she stood staring at the beauty before her. Everything was surreal.

"Escadaria Selaron, that's what the locals call these steps," he told her.

"Was it deliberate?" Chloe asked.

"Yes, they were created by Jorge Selaron, who said he wanted to give back to his people. Tiles of different colors from several parts of the world were sent to him, and this is the result. This beauty is unrivaled by anything else in Rio," Gary said.

They followed the steps, moving from Joaquim Da Silva Street to Pinto Martins. She would pause and savor the beauty before her, exclaiming as they went, her admiration growing with time.

"It must have taken the artist a long time to do this. Do you see how he made sure to make the colors all the same as the Brazilian flag?" she asked.

"Yes, I believe that was deliberate. Are you ready for the next place I want to take you to?" he asked her.

"Where is that?" she replied.

"I'm going to take you to the closest observation point that will give you a good view of Christ the Redeemer," he said.

"We saw that when we were making our descent into the city," she said.

"You haven't really seen the statue if you only saw it by air. Come on," he said, taking her hand. They drove through the Tijuca Forest and made their way toward Corcovado Mountain. She was in awe of the wildlife there and took numerous pictures. Her ladies were going to be so jealous.

When they caught a good sight of Corcovado Mountain, he stopped the vehicle, and almost like a drive-in theater, they watched the magnificent site that greeted them. They stared continually, watching what dazzled before their eyes. A smile came across Chloe's face as she stared at the colossus. Its hands were spread out, welcoming like the Statue of Liberty.

"Thanks for showing me all of these sights today," she said.

"My pleasure. Do you not remember how we enjoyed walking all around the college campus in the old days? Enjoying a sight here and another there?" he asked.

They laughed, recalling their obsession with sightseeing and the outdoors.

When they drove back to Copacabana in the evening, the ladies were all anxious to see her and learn how their trip went. Olivia mentioned that William had come around, and Chloe scoffed.

"I think you should listen to him," Olivia advised.

"No way! There was a naked woman in his bed! What do you expect him to explain to me?" she asked.

"Listening and walking away if it doesn't make sense wouldn't hurt. Just give him a chance," she advised.

"After the show, maybe. Are you guys ready for tomorrow? You aren't ready for what we have coming your way," she said.

"We can guess," Ava said.

Chloe had made her decision about William. There was no reasonable explanation for Gertrude's presence in his room, especially with her clothes off and her ample boobs. She was trying to kill whatever residual feelings she might have for him. This way, she could live her life without thinking of the men that made it hell.

***

The nightlife had improved a lot since tourists and holiday makers began to troop into Rio. Even now, the streets were lined with numerous people: laughing teenagers, happy partygoers, and couples, all making memories amongst the sands and ready to unwind after a long week. It was Friday, after all. But William didn't notice any of that. Tonight, he walked the streets aimlessly. He didn't feel hungry at all. Everything he did was almost robotic. What he really wanted was a few moments alone with Chloe. He just wanted to understand what was going on.

Today had been such a hectic day for him, with all of the tasks he had to tackle driving him nuts. He knew how to handle each task, but the short time allotted to each was causing him to be restless; that was the reason he had chosen to step out from his quarters for a while in order to clear his head. These days he found that his thoughts were easily crowded and his mind often overwhelmed by too many things. He shook his head, recalling his conversation with Henry before he had left the embassy building. Henry had wanted them to hang out at his favorite bar, but William couldn't because he had so much work to do. Maybe he should have agreed. Henry hadn't been very happy with his choice and had pestered William to have a change of heart.

"You never have any time to yourself, William. You're always in work mode. Not even on a weekend, man!" Henry had claimed.

"That's not true. I unwind when it's necessary. I just can't do it today," William had replied.

"You always have so much to do. When do you ever relax? When do you take time to have some fun?" Henry had asked.

William laughed. Henry was right. He really might have been able to get over this trouble if he could just unwind and forget, but he couldn't. He couldn't tell how it all happened, but somehow, Chloe had gotten under his skin, and he had loved her like he had never loved anyone else before.

"You're a good example of why people should never fall in love." Henry had said and smiled ruefully.

"I guess, but I still don't regret Chloe. She wasn't a mistake," William had replied. "She'll be back. You'll see."

William could espy the gothic structure where his favorite grill could be found. The sign for Carinha's Grill shone brightly in neon light placed high above the entrance door. For such a huge place, one would think its sign would be much larger than it was. The building was large, towering above the buildings beside it. The bright purple of the building always made William smile. It was such a bad mixture of paint that stood out like a sore thumb on this street. There was this feeling deep inside of him this evening.

He could feel it in the tips of his toes and climbing through his whole being until his entire body nearly shook with a kind certainty that he couldn't put his finger on. He could recall feeling the same thing each time he stood in front of this building, but his feet always brought him back here. The few times he decided to try meat somewhere else, he didn't like the taste.

Tonight felt much different from all the other nights. He didn't feel a thing. It felt like one of those days when he had to find his grilled beef in one of the other places in this neighborhood. His mouth tasted like ash, and he walked with slow, deliberate steps. A hooded silhouette lined the outer wall like a skinny tree bereft of its leaves. William thought he recognized the silhouette as being Carinha, the owner of the restaurant. William recalled him standing right there each time he came to get himself some grilled beef. Tonight, he decided to pause and have a chat with him instead of just throwing a greeting and walking in the same way he had always done.

"Good evening, Carinha." William greeted.

But it wasn't the old man. He had just met the surprise of his life: when the figure turned, a beautiful Brazilian woman with beads and cowries in her hair stared back at him. She was either in her late twenties or early thirties. His mouth flew open in surprise.

"If you leave your mouth open for much longer, a fly might make a home of it, William," she said to him.

His surprise doubled as his mouth clamped shut, and his eyes widened instead. He had never shared a word with this woman, yet she seemed to know his name.

"How . . . How do you know my name?" he asked.

"I know a lot of things, more than we have time to discuss tonight," she replied.

He looked at her. She wore an infectious smile that reminded William of his prayers. She was the kind of woman he wanted in his life. This woman before him had the mannerisms, the beauty, and a certain grace about her that made him wonder if he wasn't staring at the answer to his prayers.

"I'm not the answer to your prayers, William," she said.

"What the heck!" William exclaimed, flabbergasted at the fact that she was able to read his thoughts so clearly.

"What are you?" William asked.

"What? I'm not a thing, William. I'm a human being," she replied.

"Are you a mind reader? A witch? Or what?" he asked.

"I'm none of those. I'm only psychic," the lady said.

"I've never spoken to you before now. How did you know what I was thinking only moments ago?" he asked.

"The world is a web of interconnectedness. We are linked to each other in a network, which means we can communicate without opening our mouths. You told me your thoughts. You told me your name. And I told you mine. You just weren't listening," she explained.

"You must be a witch; that's the only explanation," William said out loud. He couldn't understand her. *What connection? What is she talking about?* William thought before realizing she must have heard all of that too.

"This doesn't happen to everybody, William. It's only happening to you now because you're a special person who deserves someone special. More will happen to you in the future. I know you doubt me. I know you don't believe anything I say to you, but I want you to promise me you won't shut off your heart to the universe. Tell me you will remain open."

He was really scared now, and the first thought to pop into his head was to turn around and get away from this woman with her crazy ideas and eerie appearance. Everything about her screamed of something out of this world. William had tons of questions swirling around his mind, but he knew he wouldn't be getting any good answers from this woman who claimed to hear a man who never opened his mouth. He turned and began to walk away, but then her voice followed him, screaming in his ears. He ran home, banging his door behind him and throwing himself on his bed when he arrived.

Somehow, when he allowed himself to think, it was Chloe he thought about. She was the one woman who brought him joy and set his body on fire.

CHAPTER 12

The Sarah Lavigne event was only one day away, and Olivia could see the excitement despite Chloe's best efforts at playing it all down. For the others, the excitement was feverish. It was almost like they were preparing for a special party of their own with the calls and the frenzy that had come over them in the past few days. Gary took Chloe to the spa the day before her big day. She got her hair, nails, and everything done. They had so much fun, the sort of fun they hadn't had in a long time.

All through the night, Gary worried himself sick. He was hoping to tell Chloe how he felt after she walked the runway.

"Are you ready?" he asked.

"Everything I need is ready. Just let me run and get it," Chloe said and ran out of Gary's room.

When Gary saw her in her dress, his eyes watered and he opened his arms to hug Chloe. He had no words, and so he expressed what he felt in the best way he knew how.

"You're going to wow them out there. Trust me," he said.

"You made it possible, Gary. Thank you so much," she replied.

"You know the only thing I did was make you think outside the box and find creative ways to perform your magic?" he said.

"I know. And I'm grateful for that," she said.

They were quiet for a few moments, retreating into their own minds with private thoughts. Chloe recalled the old days when they had always sat just like this on the eve of every competition. They had always killed it, making such powerful appearances that everything always came out magical. Some of the designers they represented were wowed at what they could do with the material they were given. "Gary, what happens now?" Chloe asked.

"What do you mean?" he responded.

"After this, no matter how it goes, what comes next?" she asked.

Gary chuckled at that question. He had similar questions about the future, about himself and her, and what might be out there for them. He didn't want to tell her his plans until tomorrow came, but now with this question, he didn't know how to respond.

"When I got into organizing and planning, I knew where to go and how to go about it. But if tomorrow is a success, how do I move forward?" she asked him.

"You have nothing to fear, Chloe. You handled everything they threw at you in college with an impressive and savvy attitude; the world won't be so hard. I mean, we've done these before," he responded.

"We were ready. We were ready to take the world by storm!" she exclaimed.

"Those were years that have come and gone. Now we start anew." Chloe grew quiet when he said this. She was all of a sudden feeling the same anger she had felt on their first meeting in Rio.

"Have you loved anyone since me?" she asked.

Gary eyed her in a suggestive way, and they both burst into laughter. He had understood the intent of Chloe's question but would choose a diversion instead of giving any details on his love life since they had been together. Chloe didn't press. She didn't trust him and his intentions, but he seemed to be useful at this time, and she had to live with that. Besides, she wasn't going to spoil this beautiful moment they were enjoying with a question about love life.

"Are you going to be staying with me tonight?" Gary asked.

"Just like the old days; we are together on the nights of the big shows." She smiled.

They spent the rest of the night talking and laughing about nothing and everything. At some point during the night, they had gone out to stare at the sky with the magnificent stars dotting the heavens. Chloe could recall younger days when she had learned the names of the stars from her father's lips. Those were the days before things changed, years of innocence before the things in her head became too muddied up. Tonight, she felt happy, Gary's boisterous spirit fell on her, and she relived those happy moments again. Her cheeks hurt from all the laughter, and she wasn't ready to stop yet. She had been feeling so much joy that she hadn't even thought about the event since they checked out the dress earlier. There was no anxiety, no fear, just joy.

Morning came fast, and they spent a good deal of the day getting ready for the event. They were at the venue, with the ladies there to give her support. She knew she was ready. She had always been ready, but being away from something she loved so much meant it would take some getting used to again.

When she walked out onto the runway, side by side with Gary, she felt confident. But then her eyes caught sight of a man in the crowd. William had a bandage on his left hand, and she was cut deep when she saw a cast on him too. She jumped off the runway, rushing toward him.

She fell to his side and held him close, her hand wrapped tightly around him. Tears fell from her eyes, and she fought them back. Several members of the crowd watched with keen interest as she rose and led William out of the room. Gary stared at them, his eyes spitting fire. When he saw them making to leave, he yelled from the runway.

"Damn you, Chloe! That walk was perfect. Why did you have to ruin it?" he asked.

"I'm sorry, I love him," she yelled back, giggling like a schoolgirl as she led him out of the room and into the lobby. "Get us a room, William," she said.

They walked to the counter and spoke to the receptionist, who handed them a key. They walked up to the room giggling like children.

"I was hoping to talk to you after the event. I wanted to know why you left without a word," he said.

"Gertrude was naked in your bed one morning when I came

to visit," she said.

"What are you talking about?" he replied.

"Don't try to deny it, William. The sight of that bandage touched a chord in my heart, but a lie will break that," she said.

"I have never touched or been with Gertrude in my life. The last time she was in my room was because she banged her shoulder and I was trying to help bandage it. Nothing else! I promise, I'm not lying," he said.

Chloe stared into his eyes; there was sincerity in them. Gertrude had been playing games before. Maybe she should have told William about the incident. She felt guilty that she hadn't. She bent and kissed him, choosing to believe him.

The kiss became as hungry as it was tender. It was like a caress, traveling gently over his lips. She latched on to his lower lip as his jacket suit found its way to the floor around his legs, leaving his upper body covered in only his white shirt. She tore at his buttons, pulling the shirt off quickly and throwing his pants off too.

She stared at his taut stomach, desire blinding her eyes. To her, his upper body could have been sculpted by Rodin, the eminent artist. She ran her hand over his abs, caressing him, sliding up and down his hairy chest as he closed his eyes.

He kissed her back, tasting her lips as she opened her mouth to let him into her. She moaned as he ate her upper lip, tasting her, his tongue roaming, rolling around hers as her hand traveled down to cup his balls, massaging them softly. His palm found her firm boob and squeezed gently, enjoying the firmness of it in his hand. His hunger rose, and he bent slowly, kissing her neck, going up to her cheek to nibble on her earlobe. She closed her eyes and savored the sweet sensations coursing through here. His hand drew a long line across her stomach that ended right on her mound as he caressed the top of her pussy, sliding through the opening and over its lips. She moaned deeply as his hand pleasured her, but she wanted to taste him, to feel his cock in her mouth.

She knelt down before him and took his whole length in her hand, caressing that taut meat and watching it pulsate in her hand. Then she bent and kissed his tip, trailing that kiss down to the end of his shaft to trace a line over his balls, making him squirm with pleasure. She kissed the length of the shaft back up to his turgid member. Then, almost as if on cue, she buried the length of his shaft in her mouth, her palm still cradling his balls and massaging that space between his balls and his anal region. He felt her warm lips encircle his large cock, and a deep moan escaped him, almost like a child whimpering. She pleasured him further, unwilling to let go as he squirmed in her hands. She was sucking on him hungrily, like one who had finally found the elusive object of her desire.

"Shit!" he moaned with his head thrown backward.

She bobbed her head up and down his shaft, running her palm up and down at the same time in a fast motion that had his legs shaking under him. He felt his orgasm coming close, so he began to thrust into her lips, fucking her mouth quickly. She rubbed a small vein behind his balls, and he felt the waves slow down. She rose off the ground and kissed him with the same lips that had just come off his cock. He could taste the saltiness on her lips, but he didn't mind. His hand rested on the small of her back, traveling lower until he laid it on her butt. He grabbed her butt and pushed her into his center, enjoying the feeling of her mound on his cock.

He pressed her against the wall, kissing her passionately as his pleasure mounted heavily. She was light in his hands, and he massaged, caressed, and kneaded all of her, slipping a finger in and running it around her pussy opening while she squirmed under him. She was dripping wet, and he could feel her juices sliding over his finger.

He swiveled her around and pushed her against the wall, not waiting for an invitation. He slid into her pussy, slamming home almost immediately as his cock found a home through her wet pussy. He grabbed a hold of her waist, thrusting deep into her. His thrust was slow, pushing his cock slowly into her and moving out slowly until only his tip was left inside her. Then he went again, slamming deep into her and making her moan.

His slow thrusts lasted only a moment, and then he went faster.

Thrusting deep into her pussy as she moaned and screamed in ecstasy. She was bucking back into him, thrusting back as he thrust into her, their bodies moving like the lyrics of a good song: coherent, ordered, and in sync. His palm traveled up her side, grabbing hold of her boob, pinching her nipple as he slammed into her from behind.

He pushed her against the wall again, with his cock still lodged inside of her. She moaned louder with each thrust, and he could feel the pleasure of her pussy caressing his cock in that tight embrace. He turned her around to face him, lifting one of her legs while she bent the other slightly, her pussy staring him in the face.

He slid into her, thrusting deep and fast again with one of her legs hanging on his shoulder while he slammed in. She was moaning deeply, enjoying each thrust of his cock deep into her orifice. He placed his thumb against her clit and rubbed it hard while he thrust into her, watching her face go wild as the pleasure tore through her. Her legs began to quiver under her as the first wave of her orgasm tore through her. She came screaming his name at the top of her lungs.

He bent to run his tongue lightly up her pussy, lapping up all her juices. He was all desire now, all of his inhibitions thrown out the window as he sucked momentarily on her pussy. She moaned as his tongue on her pussy triggered another orgasm, her juices covering his face.

He pushed her down to her knees on the bed and knelt behind her, positioning his cock over her pussy again. As he slid back into her wet pussy, she moaned and arched her back further, allowing him better access. He began to thrust in slowly, moving his cock in and out of her. When he thrust into her now, he thrust like one possessed. He went hard and fast, his hand grabbing her waist tight as he tore into her.

He went hard at her pussy, his thumb slipping into her asshole at one point. She moaned as the thumb found her hole, the pleasure climbing a notch higher as he slammed into her. The slap of his pelvis against her ass and the moans coming from their lips were like poetry, an ode dedicated to pleasure. He didn't want to stop, his initial tempo lost in the staccato that was going on at the moment.

"I'm going to cum," he announced.

She sucked him off, cleaning him quickly, making sure no errant cum had gone to waste. Then she rose and kissed his lips, making him taste himself on her lips again.

They lay on the bed in each other's arms. She picked gently at his hairy chest, wondering what she had just done. Then realizing that it didn't really matter, she poured a glass of wine for herself and another for him and handed his glass to him.

"Some people say that wine is an aphrodisiac," she said, winking at him. He drank without commenting, enjoying the sight of her naked body, exquisite and without a blemish. "Do you know what I mean by aphrodisiac?" she asked with that mischievous look on her face.

He understood now, and a smile broke out on his face. He wanted more of her just as she wanted more of him too. They were both still as naked, and he admired her impeccable body. She had made an exceptional sight on runways, and as he watched her now, he felt she didn't get as good a rating as she should have. He felt his cock rising to the sight, her ass just inches away from his palm.

He stretched out his hand and squeezed her ass. She felt her body tingle and drew toward him, feeling that animal desire rising to the surface.

"Spank my ass," she said. He slapped it, watching it jiggle to his touch and her excited reaction as she felt his slap. She giggled like a schoolgirl discovering sex for the first time. He turned her around and raised a hand to her cheeks, pulling her toward him. He kissed her lips passionately, and she responded, opening up to let him in. She sucked on his lower lip, their tongues dovetailing each other. They were feeling each other up, enjoying how their lips felt in communion.

His palm caressed her body, traveling all over her, squeezing her flesh, singing pleasures through her. He picked her up in his powerful arms and laid her on the small couch. Then he bent over her boobs and began to sing pleasures to them, taking a mouthful of her nipple and sucking gently, biting down softly, listening to her exhale with pleasure. He wrapped one palm over one boob while his mouth sang pleasures to her other nipple. He alternated, moving from one boob to the other, sucking, pinching, and kneading so that the pleasures sailed through every zone.

He kissed down her stomach, going over her belly button, running his tongue in a pleasurable circle. He traveled lower, pausing to kiss the top of her mound, blowing softly over the top and kissing the spot while his palm caressed her inner thighs. He went past her mound, kissing her inner thighs, traveling past her pussy and traveling down to kiss her legs. He worshipped her skinny legs, biting her knee and going further down until he took her toes in his mouth, sucking the partings, singing pleasures into her.

He traveled back up, following the other leg, kissing even harder, enjoying the moans and gasps that escaped her. He neared her pussy, planting kisses all over her thighs while his palms caressed her tenderly. When his finger parted her pussy lips, moving over her hole tenderly, she arched back and gasped, and when he slipped a finger into her, going deep into her pussy, she moaned, arching her back with the unexpected pleasure. He kissed the top of her mound, sucking on her exposed clit, lapping softly against her pussy while his finger kept sliding in and out. He latched onto her pussy, sucking hard, his tongue running over all of her while she squirmed with the pleasure she couldn't keep away. She moaned, her legs rising to form a prison for his neck.

He wasn't thinking of leaving anyway. He poured the wine from his glass over her flat tummy and watched it slide down toward her pussy. He sucked on it, lapping it all up quickly as she moaned deeply with the pleasure of his motions. He could feel her orgasm coming quickly as she began to thrash about on the couch, her hand seeking an anchor. He intensified the finger action, introducing another finger as he lapped against her pussy in quick motion.

When she came, she screamed his name, holding tight to the couch. He didn't allow her to come down from that cloud of pleasure. He thrust into her even while she was still at that peak, and she moaned deeply, his hard thrust triggering another orgasm. He paused, savoring the feeling of his cock back into her warm orifice. He began to thrust into her again, slamming slowly, moving with ease in and out of her wet pussy. He watched his cock slide in and out until all that was left inside her was his tip.

He went faster, his thumb rubbing her exposed clit as he fucked her. He bent over and took her nipple in his mouth as he slammed into her. He threw all his restraint off and slammed deep into her, going faster. There was no rhythm, no music. He was fucking her hard until she screamed with the onset of another orgasm. He liked the look on her face when her orgasm hit her; it was almost like she was feeling the pleasure in the deepest parts of her.

She pressed a hand on his chest and pushed him back. He lay on his back and waited for her. She positioned herself over his cock and impaled herself on it. She began to bounce up and down, pushing forward and backward, her hand planted backward on the edge of his belly. They were both moaning, the pleasure increasing further as she began to grind into his cock, moving in a circle. She went back to bouncing up and down on him, going hard and fast until he felt her pause, her body vibrating over his cock.

He was up in a flash, laying her on her back. His torso was the perfect height. He sat her on the bed and bent to kiss her pussy, sucking for only a moment before burying his cock deep into her once more. She moaned as he penetrated her pussy once more, slamming in and out of her speedily. He wasn't wasting any time. He slammed into her again, thinking of nothing else but the pleasure that was coursing through him. Her hand rested on his chest, caressing his nipples, squeezing as his cock sang pleasures to her pussy.

He then got her off the bed and positioned her over the arm of the couch, her ass lifting slightly up in the air, just at the right angle for him to find his way home. He thrust in, his palms going round to grab a hold of her boobs as he slammed home, thrusting slowly in and out of her while he worked her nipples and kneaded her boobs.

"Fuck me harder!" she called. He held her waist now and thrust into her, going hard and fast until she climaxed again. He wasn't ready to cum yet, so he held his orgasm back, thrusting slower, pacing himself and managing to hold back the wave of his orgasm. He wanted to look into her eyes when he shot his load this time, so he flipped her around, still holding her over the arm of the couch. He thrust back into her in that faux missionary position. His cock slammed in deep, and he stared into her eyes. Then she closed her eyes and savored the feeling of his sweet cock traveling through her.

***

In the dark, they walked along the shore, holding hands. For Chloe, the stars above were cheering them on, the atmosphere itself was palpable with their love, and even the waves slapping against each other felt like a confirmation of their affection.

She recalled how everyone who had come before had left, how the distance had always stolen her lovers from her, and it made her worry that it might do the same here. She didn't want that.

"Will you always be here in Rio? Or will they move you about from city to city?" she asked.

"Why? Do you want to come along?" he asked instead. She looked away. She wouldn't mind that one bit; her life wasn't static. She could be a model anywhere, even in dangerous places.

"Maybe. Are you asking?" she responded.

"No, I wouldn't want you moving all the time because of me," he said. "I'll be resigning from my position. I've paid my dues, and now it's time to go home," he continued. Chloe's heart was bursting with happiness. She had found herself a man who wanted her enough to quit his job.

"Where's home for you? New York? Vegas?" she asked him.

"Home is you, Chloe," he said.

EPILOGUE

William told her everything later, when their passion was spent and they had gone down to the bar for drinks. He narrated how they had driven out to meet the terrorists at the foot of Sugarloaf Mountain.

It was during the ensuing shoot-out that he had sustained the injury to his arm. And due to this injury, he would have to take a compulsory leave of absence.

"What will you do if you quit the army?" she asked.

"I have a few ideas, but I'll be fine. I have an inheritance large enough to keep me buoyant for as long as I want. Haven't you wondered how I'm able to pay for your hotel and the other luxuries in my life?" he asked.

"No, I haven't," she said.

"I'll show you when we return home, but now I just want to leave Rio, head to someplace else and spend some quality time with you!" he said. "Tell me, where would you like to head off to?" he asked.

"How about the Maldives?" she asked.

"Now, that is a beautiful place to go!" Olivia said, falling into an empty seat at their table.

"I'm so sorry for how I acted, Liv. You were just trying to help," Chloe said.

"It's okay. Just know that if I ever have to step in to help you again, I'll still do it without hesitation," Olivia said.

"I wouldn't have it any other way," Chloe replied.

"Have you seen Avery and Henry? They've been most inseparable since last night," Olivia whispered.

"You're kidding! Henry is..." William began, then caught himself.

"He is what?" the ladies asked.

"Nothing, that's all I'm saying," William quipped.

It means the world to me that you brought my book. Writing is my passion and I look forward to hearing from you.

So if you liked this book, I'd like to ask for a small favor. Would you be so kind to leave a review on Amazon? It'd be very much appreciated!

Misty Rosette

p.s. A review is like a warm hug to us authors – we love it!

Love in The Caribbean (Love and Travel Series Book 3)

Jamaica holds lots of surprises… and secrets have a way of getting out.

With my wedding with William on the horizon, I thought that an island getaway would be the perfect recipe for letting loose and celebrating my happily ever after.

But things aren't as perfect as they seem. William is hiding a big secret from me… and it might just blow our entire relationship apart.

Things are heating up on this beautiful island, and my girlfriends are going wild – and after William's best friend Craig comes to calm things down, Mia catches his eye.

So while I'm left struggling to know if I can trust William after everything that's happened, Craig is scheming how to win Mia's heart.

Our wedding is hanging in the balance, and I'm afraid of getting my heart broken. Can I find it in me to forgive William for his past? Or is our love story doomed to end here?

And what will become of Mia and the dashing, handsome suitor Craig?

ABOUT THE AUTHOR

I am a hopeless romantic. Since childhood, I have always been interested in romantic tv series, novels, shows, etc. Also, I have been an avid reader since the age of 3. When everyone around me was busy playing, my comfort space had always been in books. When I was a teenager, instead of shopping and making new friends, I would happily make myself comfortable and dive into a book.

This is the reason why I decided to capture my imagination onto paper and begin my journey as a romance author. It is my hope that you will have enjoyed my unique romantic stories, and stay with me as I continue to pour my heart into my writing.

FREE GIFT

Sign up to my mailing list to receive an exclusive free novella, and be notified on any new releases, giveaways, contests, cover reveals and so much more!

https://dl.bookfunnel.com/kguy19f0uw

Is he just a holiday fling… or a soulmate beyond her wildest dreams?

My name is Olivia, and I've got no job, no partner, and nothing to look forward to. I could end it right there, but despite all of that, cupid works in mysterious ways.

When my girlfriends suggested a spontaneous trip to one of the most romantic cities on the planet, I could hardly refuse. The beautiful waterways of Venice might be hiding the man of my dreams… or at least they'll take my mind off my bad luck.

But I can't shake the feeling my friends are hiding something from me. I don't have much time to think about it – because now I find myself falling for someone, I never thought I would…

Is this nothing more than a holiday fling? Or could it blossom into something much more than I ever could have imagined? I guess there's only one way to find out.